BENEATH
HER
SKIN

C. S. PORTER

A KES MORRIS FILE

Vagrant
PRESS

Vagrant Press is an imprint of
Nimbus Publishing Limited
3660 Strawberry Hill Street, Halifax, NS, B3K 5A9
(902) 455-4286 nimbus.ca

Printed and bound in Canada
NB1588

Editor: Whitney Moran
Design: Jenn Embree

This story is a work of fiction. Names, characters, incidents, and places, including organizations and institutions, are used fictitiously.

Library and Archives Canada Cataloguing in Publication

Title: Beneath her skin : a Kes Morris file / C.S. Porter.
Names: Porter, C. S. (Author of Beneath her skin), author.
Identifiers: Canadiana (print) 20210216794
Canadiana (ebook) 20210216832 | ISBN 9781771089814 (softcover)
ISBN 9781771089999 (EPUB)
Classification: LCC PS8631.O7325 B46 2021 | DDC C813/.6—dc23

Nimbus Publishing acknowledges the financial support for its publishing activities from the Government of Canada, the Canada Council for the Arts, and from the Province of Nova Scotia. We are pleased to work in partnership with the Province of Nova Scotia to develop and promote our creative industries for the benefit of all Nova Scotians.

I.

HARRISON HOLLERED UPSTAIRS, "IF YOU'RE NOT DOWN IN TWO MINUTES I'm leaving without you—and I bloody well mean it." It wasn't getting any easier with that kid. Fourteen and all the attitude. He slapped two sausages between a folded waffle and headed to the truck.

It was a perfect Sunday. The long, dismal trudge of winter was over and a true spring day had arrived. It smelled green and alive. Maybe this summer he'd get the house painted. A good project for him and Mac. Get him out of his room.

He fired up the old pickup and it grumbled to a start. He could smell burning oil. He should trade it in, but he'd had it since before Mac was born, and it had never failed him.

He wasn't good at waiting and started to count. He made it to twelve before his son came through the front door pulling a hoodie over his head and almost tripped down the steps. Mac got in and slammed the door.

"Not so hard." Harrison could hear the badgering in his voice. He just wanted them to have a good day. "Here, eat something." He handed over the waffle sandwich.

"Dad, it's not even fucking eight yet."

"You don't have to swear all the time," Harrison said as he backed out of the driveway.

"Like you and Mom?"

Harrison took the swipe. He got it: Mac was angry and wanted his father to hurt as much as he did. As if he wasn't. Divorce left a wide swath of collateral damage. This whole

3

morning was about making time for them to hang out and forget the hard stuff. He tried to restart: "Look at the day. Perfect. Remember how it poured last year?"

Mac swallowed a yawn. "I don't even like shooting."

"Since when? You begged me for a .22 when you were six. You constantly play that video game and it's shooting all the time."

Harrison looked out to the first warming sun of the season. Soon the trees would bud. Spring always felt hopeful to him, like another chance. "It's good for us to get out, Mac. Do something physical, something real. Could be we win it this year. How great would that be?"

Mac slumped down in his seat and chewed on the waffle like it was cardboard. He rolled down his window and, when he thought his father wasn't looking, dropped it onto the road. Harrison decided to let it go. He was the same at that age.

"Remember to keep the butt tight to your shoulder, take a breath, aim, then gently exhale while you take the shot. Try to imagine yourself and the rifle as one, and you're the foundation holding it solid to the earth. And when you squeeze the trigger, don't jerk or flinch. One fluid motion. Right?"

"Yeah. I remember."

They pulled onto a dirt track that lead to the Rod and Gun Club. Dust flew up behind them and gravel popped under the vehicle. Mac stared out the window watching the trees stream by and squinted his eyes until they blurred into one continuous, shapeless movement.

They parked by the members' club, which was really just a cabin, and headed to the back of the truck. Other father-and-son teams were already milling about, making their way towards the wooden tables set up along the front of the shooting range. Harrison clapped Mac on the back as he lowered the tailgate exposing their rifle, clad in a deep brown leather sheath. "Let's show 'em what we got."

"A family falling to shit?"

Harrison's shoulders slumped; that one hurt. "I'm trying, Mac. I really am."

"Sorry." And Harrison knew he was.

He handed Mac the rifle. "It's all yours." It was the first time he had let him carry it to the line, and he could see the flush of pride in his son. His boy would soon be a young man. A thought that baffled Harrison.

Large, round hay bales had been placed between the firing line and the permanent targets to shorten the distance for the kids—not by much, just enough to give them a chance at a bull's eye. Harrison would love to see Mac outshoot the private-school brats, decked out in their camo pants and open-fingered leather gloves. Being a cop's kid made him an outsider. That, and money.

"Harrison!"

Mac looked at his dad and they gave each other an *Oh, crap* look.

"What a morning, hey? Got that goin' for us."

Harrison faked a smile, "Hey, John. Quite a change from last year, that's for sure." John Howzer was a big man, not just in size, but arrogant and rich. He had a "summer cottage" in the area. Harrison's entire house could fit in its living room. He'd had to call him twice about his kid's underage drinking. "You remember Mac?"

"Of course. Grown a hell of a lot since last year. Wow." He made a fake punch at Mac's abs and Mac's fist clenched. The guy's laugh was as artificial as his tan. "You ready to shoot?"

"Yes, sir. I'm going to go get set up, Dad." Behind Howzer's back, Mac grinned and flashed a middle finger.

Little shit, Harrison thought, and gave his son a thumbs-up. "I'll be right with you." He hurriedly gathered the rest of their gear.

"They grow up fast," Howzer said. "Mine's going to be out-shooting me soon."

Harrison slung the strap of his binoculars over his neck and slammed the tailgate shut. He'd had enough of Howzer.

"You're still using those? I just invested in a new pair." Howzer lifted the military-grade binoculars from his chest. "10x56 with the most amazing image stabilizers. Bought them for the boat this summer, but thought I'd try them out today. Have a look."

Howzer had been fondling the binoculars since he approached, waiting to be asked about his latest toy. Harrison hated to engage, but he was curious. The binoculars were light and perfectly balanced. Harrison focused on Mac, who appeared close enough to touch. He could see the loose stitches around the shoulder of his shirt. He didn't want to be impressed, but he was.

"Expensive?"

"You don't want to know."

Their team would have a decided advantage. Harrison handed back the binoculars, leaving a thumbprint on the eyepiece. "Well, good luck, John."

"No luck needed." He headed off, nodding at everyone he passed. Lord of the Range. That guy got under Harrison's skin. He shook it off. He wasn't going to let that asshole ruin their day. He joined Mac at the lineup.

Mac had drawn the first lot. The four boys wrote their names on their targets, and a judge headed to the bales to pin them up. Two other judges in white coats placed boxes of shells on the chalk line. Mac was starting in lane three.

The mic crackled and the announcer welcomed the crowd and thanked their sponsors. He called out the names of the shooters on line and there was a smattering of applause. "All right. Fathers, stand behind your sons while you spot. You will be allowed to talk to your boys. Do not touch them or their rifle. You have ten shells in front of you. When I say 'make ready,' you will load. Always point your muzzle to the ground until you are ready to fire. Do not fire until you hear the buzzer."

Harrison winked encouragement when Mac turned around. "You got this."

They both put on their earmuffs and safety glasses.

"All right, lads. Make ready."

The four boys loaded their guns and stared down the range in anticipation.

"Take aim."

Their rifles raised. Harrison glanced to the other fathers coaching their sons. Beside him, John had his high-end binoculars up and was barking orders: "Spread your legs. Stop squeezing the grip..." Harrison merely leaned in close to his son's earmuff and whispered, "Don't forget to breathe."

Mac took a breath and grounded himself. The buzzer sounded and loud reports and smoke filled the bright sky. Harrison glanced to John, who was not pleased with his kid's first volley. Mac was doing just fine, calmly reloading and taking steady aim.

Harrison checked his son's target through his scratched binoculars' lenses, which blurred and marred the focus. "Half a degree up, a degree left." Mac pulled the trigger. Bull's eye. Harrison suppressed his excitement and kept his voice calm. "Perfect. That's the line."

When the pressure was on, Mac always rose to the occasion. He was smart and calm, a thinker, and he could shoot. Maybe someday he would join the force. Nothing would make Harrison prouder.

He noticed something on his lens obscuring the corner of Mac's target. He panned over, but the smudge remained. He tried to focus on it, but his crappy binoculars couldn't manage the distance. He shifted back to the bull's eye to vaguely catch Mac's next shot find dead centre. Harrison checked the bottom edge again. There was definitely something on the paper. Something red.

"John. I need your binoculars for a second."

"Screw you," Howzer shouted back over the gunfire. "Work with what you have."

"I'm not asking." Harrison yanked the strap over John's neck, snagging his earmuffs. "Sorry, mate."

"Interference! Judge!" Howzer hollered and his hand shot up in protest.

Harrison zoomed in on the target and the image snapped into focus: a widening bloom, bright as fresh blood. "Hold your fire! Stop shooting!" He waved to a judge. "Stop the competition!"

John's kid's shot went wide and his father was mouthing off: "That last shot shouldn't count!" The buzzer sounded and the boys put their rifles in safe position.

Mac turned on his father. "What the hell, Dad?"

"Stay there." Harrison strode into the range towards the hay bales, ignoring the parents' outcries and his son's embarrassment. One of the judges ran after him, an older man whom Harrison didn't know. Harrison pulled out his badge from under his shirt. "Give me a minute."

He went directly to Mac's bale. Wet, red patches were widening across the paper target. He looked to the other targets. One other was stained. He moved cautiously to the back of the bale and saw a series of thin sticks stuck in the hay, barely noticeable. They reminded him of nailheads. When he stepped back, he could see a woven seam. He extracted a stick from the bottom corner and the hay unhitched. A hand flopped out.

Straw pricked Harrison's fingernails and scratched his wrists as he ripped away the rest of the skewers and tore at the plug of hay. It fell to the ground intact. Inside, crammed in the cavity, was an older man. Naked. On his knees. Hands behind his back. Wrists bound. The soles of his feet blistered and caked with dirt. There weren't any exit wounds on his back. A trickle of blood was seeping around his contorted legs. He had been stuffed in to face the firing line. It almost looked like he was praying.

Harrison checked the man's wrist. The flesh was warm. He couldn't find a pulse, but he already knew the man was dead by the stillness of the ribs and the three bull's-eye shots lined up with his head.

He looked down the range to his fourteen-year-old son, still a boy, not even in high school yet.

His heart beating fear, Harrison ran to the next bale.

II.

KES TOSSED HER OVERNIGHT BAG ON THE PASSENGER SEAT AND STARTED her old Jaguar XJ6. It purred awake. The car was the only thing her father had left her in his will, but that was just fine with her; it was a thing of beauty. She pulled out of her driveway and headed for the quickest route to the highway south.

Wincing, she pulled her shoulders back and arched her neck side to side. Early morning Pilates had been rough, like the instructor had been angry about something. But here she was at thirty-eight, confident she was in the best shape of her life. There had been a man at the studio, a friend of her instructor, who'd asked her if she'd be interested in modelling a new line of women's exercise clothing.

"I'm a police detective," she'd told him.

"And I'm one of the Pope's cardinals," he'd replied. He offered her two thousand dollars a day, but Kes was not, nor had she ever been, the sort of girl who could be bought. She had smiled her brightest smile and told him to fuck off.

So now here she was, Kes Morris, Special Investigations Unit—Homicide Detective, driving to a small town at the behest of her captain to investigate a murder, earning far less than two thousand dollars a day. But she was doing what she was good at, something she had earned.

She was thankful it was Sunday morning. The road was wide open and she shifted up a gear. She reached into her coat pocket, found the vial of pills, popped the lid, and shook one into her palm. *Down the hatch*, she thought as she swallowed. She no longer needed them for pain; her dislocated shoulder had healed. She just liked how they made her feel. They quieted her mind from the chatter of other cases. One pill seemed to filter the constant barrage of details that others didn't seem to notice—like the twenty-two highway signs she had passed, two flattened porcupines, and seven coffee cups in the ditch—so she could focus on what was actually important. Her father said it was a gift to remember everything. She wasn't so sure. There were so many things she'd like to forget. She checked her watch. The pill would kick in about when she arrived.

She rolled down her window and breathed in the salt air. She nudged the speedometer higher. The bird's-eye maple dash and interior chrome gleamed. Kes's father had been a bit like this car. Tough, solid, and could take the sharpest corners but still stay on the road. And both had an unusual, attractive look about them. Classic, is how she would describe them. The car had been his best self—his indulgence, his escape. His happiness.

He'd always wanted a son, another detective in the family. He hadn't imagined that his daughter could fulfill his dream. Old school, that way. Yet he told her his stories, wanting her to know who he was and what he had seen. Or maybe he just needed to speak it and she was the only one there. He died before she made the force.

Growing up, she'd sit with him by the firepit listening to him explain his secrets to becoming a great investigator. Not just a good one, a great one. Night was when he talked more. He'd tell her about how you had to put on the skin of your suspect. Think like them. Taste what they desired. But after you caught your prey, he warned, you had to tear off that skin and find the beauty of things again. That was one of the secrets. She was six when she first heard that lesson.

There were things her father hadn't told her. He didn't tell her how much it would hurt. Or that there would always be bits left behind that couldn't be shed, embedded under nails and bur-rowed into pores. He hadn't told her that sometimes, she would want to keep a piece for herself. But maybe that was just her. She wished she could ask him. She shifted to fifth and could feel the worn leather of the gear stick shaped by her father's palm. She wondered about the skin she would be putting on today and felt the chafe of those she had worn before.

Unlike her father she didn't carry a weapon, preferring to trust her instincts rather than rely on a bullet to save her. Increasingly though, she was being pressured by her captain to arm herself. But she worried she'd reach for it in fear, overriding all her other senses.

The highway slipped by quickly. Long drives were always faster when she was thinking. She took the exit and hit Route 323, pushing the speed limit on the secondary road until she saw the sign for the gun club. She geared down and drove slowly along the gravel road that led to the range. She didn't want to ding her car after the new paint job. It had cost a small fortune to find someone who could match its original British Racing Green, but she wasn't one to compromise.

She turned the last corner and saw a group of men clustered around a muddied truck by the clubhouse. Some were smoking, others were eating sandwiches. It looked like a friggin' social gathering. She parked and crossed the field, making note of the starting-line tables, abandoned clipboards, and earplugs littering the ground. She headed directly to the men.

"What the hell's going on here? This is a crime scene."

An older, hawkish man with an odd, stilted gait stepped forward. He reminded her of a heron, except for the paunch of his belly. "Yeah it is, and I'm a detective," he said.

"Why isn't this scene secured?" Kes was fuming and a bit edgy from the pill, the way she liked it. But her voice was even and commanding.

"Let's slow this down, okay? I've just arrived myself. I'm Detective Brownley, and who the hell are you?"

"Detective Kes Morris. Major Crimes Division. Homicide, City Branch." She flashed her badge.

"Kes Morris...?" She could see the flash of recognition in

his eyes. She hated that her reputation preceded her. Good or bad.

"I thought you would be much older, I mean...you don't look..." Brownley tried to recover. "It's an honour to meet you." He extended his hand, which she ignored.

"I was called here to head this up by your captain. Where's Ike and Louise?

Brownley stood up straighter, surprised she knew his former colleagues and embarrassed he had misread her. "Ike had a brain aneurysm. Louise quit, went north to work on an icebreaker. Better pay, less risk."

Kes looked at him, trying to decide if what he'd said was a feeble attempt at humour or he was just an idiot. "Brownley." She said his name like he was on the shit list.

"That's right."

"And who the hell are these people?"

"Friends of mine."

Idiot. Her first impression had been right. "Get them away from my crime scene, if there's anything left of it, and tell your *friends* to vacate the scene carefully, try not to destroy whatever evidence is left."

He offered a feeble defense, "The bodies were already gone when I got here, I didn't think—"

"No, you didn't." She stepped in closer. She was shorter than him, but he had to resist the urge to step back. "Clear them out." She headed into the range toward the bales.

Brownley went to the men and Kes could see him nodding in her direction. The others looked towards her. She ignored them and began scanning the ground. There were so many fresh footprints in the soft spring mud she worried there wouldn't be any clues left to be found. She stopped in front of the bales; the paper targets had been removed. She slid her finger into one of the pocked holes and felt an empty cavity through the straw. The bodies must have been loaded in the bales somewhere else and brought here. A local farm, maybe? She pulled a small black notebook from her jacket pocket, a new one at the beginning of every case, and wrote down *Where did the hay come from?*

She walked behind the bales and studied the openings. Two had been hollowed out to leave just enough room for a body. On the ground were cut-out straw plugs with thin wood laminate attached so they wouldn't fall apart. She knelt to look more carefully at the hollowed-out opening. The edge was clean and tight. She jotted in her book—*Chainsaw?* That would take time, privacy, and planning. She registered the blood staining the ground and scattering of thin, whittled sticks. She sensed Brownley behind her and stood up.

"Are they gone?"

"Yes, sir. Ma'am." Brownley was contrite, as he should be. He tried to explain: "It was my day off. After the shitty winter we had, this was the first sunny weekend in months. We were fishing when the call came in..."

She didn't care. "Could a chainsaw have done this? Cut these portions out of one of these tight bales? Wouldn't the cut section just unravel?" Kes pulled at the bloody straw.

Brownley considered. "I could ask my partner to test one. Chester, he's good with saws. Built his own cabin."

"Where's he now?" she asked as she headed to the next bale.

"Left early this morning for his cabin."

"Call him in."

"I don't know if he has cellphone reception back there..."

Kes shot him a look.

"Yes, ma'am. I'll get on it."

Kes stepped back to get a wider view of the four bales, the two with now-empty cavities and the other two intact.

"Do we know if the victims were dead before the shooting started?"

"I heard one, a female, was still breathing. Barely. They airlifted her to the city."

"Get ahold of your partner. I don't care how. Tell him to

meet you as soon as he can. You two start with chainsaw tests. I want to know how these cuts were made. What kind of blade and how much skill it takes. Where the bales came from. And get a members list from the rod and gun club before you leave. Here's my number," she said passing him a card. "What was the name of the officer who was here with his son?"

"Harrison. Cooper Harrison."

"Where's he now?"

"Home, I'm guessing. His boy, Mac, was on the shooting line. A terrible—"

"Where does he live? I'm going to want to have a chat with him." She was warming up to Brownley. He had compassion, at least.

"On the other side of the hill. Towards the back harbour. Green Street. I don't know the number. He drives an old red pickup with an antenna on the roof."

"All right." Kes slid her notebook into her back pocket and looked at the detective head-on. "You and I kicked it off pretty bad here, Brownley. Let's get on track now, okay? We'll meet at the station at eighteen-hundred hours tonight, and every night until this over."

She headed to her car, pausing at the tables on her way, stopping at firing lane three. She ran her fingers along the chalk line, took note of the empty .22LR shell boxes. She added them to the other crime scene details sifting through her mind as she watched an osprey drift overhead.

"Detective," Brownley gently interrupted, "I've lost my ride. Think you can drop me at the station?"

Kes waved for him to follow. She got in her car, tossed her bag on the back seat, and had it started before he got in.

"Nice car."

She glanced to his muddy boots. He was still looking for the seat belt when she slipped the car into gear. Her tires spun on the grass. On the way out, she spotted four other hay bales sitting in the woods along the edge of a logging cut. She braked.

"Does the club keep a stock of these? Or were they just brought in for the competition?"

"I'm not sure. I hadn't noticed them on my way in." He was failing in every way today. "I'll add it my list."

Kes knew how she could come across; she wasn't trying to embarrass him, she was inviting him in. "So maybe someone comes here, moves these bales off the range, and replaces them with ones loaded with the bodies. Lot of bloody effort went into this. How much does a bale like that weigh?"

"Five to six hundred pounds?"

"Not something you just roll around. This has been well planned. And to have children pull the trigger..."

"Sick bastard," Brownley muttered.

"Aren't they all." Kes pulled away.

Brownley ran his fingers over the polished wood. "My son runs a car wash just behind the laundromat, paying his way through university. Tell him I sent you and he'll take care of the mud."

She glanced to the floor mat. He was holding up his feet, so as not to dirty it more.

III.

After dropping Brownley off at the station, Kes went to find Harrison.

She drove along the town's main street leading to the back harbour. Though the summer season hadn't started yet, the narrow road was already teeming with tourists visiting the galleries, restaurants, and curio shops. One day of sun and people were already fevered. Shopping had never been something Kes enjoyed, but she would love to be sitting on one of the outdoor patios sipping a cold beer.

She turned up a steep hill, past an impressive old inn that was formerly a sea captain's house. This was a wealthy town, proud of its fishing, boatbuilding, and rum-running heritage. The demographic had been shifting in recent years to foreign investors and summer residents who were buying up the coast and driving prices beyond the reach of locals. That fine line of needing tourists to survive, but at a cost that might be too high. The locals still had a reputation of being fiercely independent and, despite their friendly charm, wouldn't hesitate to tell an outsider to bugger off.

She found Green Street and slowed to admire its brightly painted, immaculately maintained Victorian houses and tidy yards. The street ended in a cul-de-sac that backed onto a hardwood lot. She spotted the red pickup with an antenna and pulled over. In the driveway beside the truck, a rusted bike leaned against a basketball hoop. The house was smaller and more modest than the others. The north side's cedar shakes were in the process of being meticulously restored.

The door was open and she rapped on the wooden screen.

"Who is it?" a voice called from a back room.

"Kes Morris. Here to have a word with Cooper Harrison."

"Not here."

"Detective Kes Morris."

A man appeared in the hallway and looked hard at her. He was solid, muscular, and stood with his feet grounded on the wide wooden planks. She instinctively made visual notes. *Athletic. A slight greying at his temples. Blue eyes. Small scar on his chin. Wiping his hands on a tea cloth.*

"No, you're not," he said. "We don't have a Morris. Or a woman. I'm not talking to reporters. Go the fuck away."

"I was brought up from the city to lead this investigation. Call Captain Puck if you'd like. I just wanted to ask you a few questions."

He stepped forward and pushed open the screen door. She could see now that he looked tired. His plaid shirt was covered with flour. He brushed his cheek and left a white smear.

"Sorry about that," he said. "The local papers been calling and I've got nothing to say to them."

Kes knew how the media could feed on the vulnerable.

"I was told you were at the scene with your son. Is he home?"

Harrison stepped out, closing the door behind him. "He's upstairs playing a video game with a pal." He leaned against the porch support and watched Kes carefully as though assessing her, wondering if she was someone he could trust. "I don't want him part of this. He doesn't know anything that I can't tell you."

"Is there somewhere we can talk?"

Harrison indicated the bench across the road, overlooking the harbour. He led the way and as he passed her, she could smell beer on his breath.

They sat at opposite ends and stared out at the water. A scallop dragger was slowly approaching a dock. Its horn sounded.

Harrison took a breath. "What do you want to know?"

Kes appreciated his matter-of-fact calm. Brownley had told her Harrison was a ten-year veteran. A good cop. By the book. Someone you could depend on. But small-town precincts were known to be tight-knit and protective of their own. She set her notebook on her lap and opened it to a blank page.

"Did you notice anything out of place when you arrived at the range this morning?"

"It was just a bunch of fathers and sons getting ready for the competition. People were excited to be out." He put his hands on his knees. They were big hands, nicked and scarred, the hands of someone who liked making things for himself.

"Your son was shooting and you were..."

"Standing behind him. Marking. We were the first group on line. I've already told all this to the guys on scene."

"But you haven't told me."

He sat back like she was pulling rank on him. And she was.

"I was looking through my binoculars at Mac's target to see if his sights were good. He had taken his first shot when I noticed something on the bottom edge of his target. I have shit binoculars, so I took John's, the guy next to me, and when I focused in, I knew it was blood. I called for the judge to stop the competition. I thought maybe an animal had been scooped up when the tractor made its pass. But the hay would have been baled last fall, so there wouldn't be fresh blood. I was just trying to make sense of it..."

He was reciting the details like he was reading it from his police notepad.

"As I approached the bales, I could see the same type of stain on the target beside Mac's. I went to his bale first and then around back of it. There wasn't any sound." He paused. "Even the birds were quiet. I saw the straw plug held in place by sticks, like needles."

"How many?"

"Eight. Thin. Maybe eight inches long. Hand-shaved. I pulled them out and saw a male victim...couldn't find a pulse. Then I went to the next bale. There was a woman inside, still alive. I tried to apply pressure, but there were too many wounds." He was looking down, and she knew he was seeing the woman. He blinked and pushed it away. "It was strange that there weren't any exit wounds. I stayed until the team arrived, then stepped back and took my son home."

Kes jotted down notes. "Did anyone seem out of place when you arrived?"

"No. We were all focused on our kids. I was just happy to get Mac out of the house. It's been such a long, crappy winter. This was supposed to be something fun for us to do together."

"Was your wife there?"

Harrison looked at her sharply and then quickly away. "She's not in the picture." He stared hard at the harbour.

"Would your son..." She checked her notes, "Mac—"

"He doesn't know anything." The line was drawn hard between them.

"Does he know..." She searched for gentler words. "...what was in the bales?"

"You mean that he shot a man? No. I don't know how to tell him that yet." He looked to his hands. Kes could see his eyes were glassy. "How do I tell him that? What kind of animal has a kid pull the trigger?" He abruptly stood and took a few steps towards the water. He swiped at his eyes.

"Your son didn't kill anyone," Kes said quietly. "Whoever set this up is the killer." She knew her words were an empty solace, but what else could she say?

Harrison swung around. "I need to be on this case, Detective." He said it as though it was an ordinary case request and not the desperate plea of a father.

Kes understood his desire, but he was a liability. "You're too close and you're not a detective."

"I've completed the sergeant's exam online. Passed with honours. My application is with the department in the city. I can apprentice under you. My captain will vouch for me." He broke from his professional pitch. "I owe it to my son to find this bastard."

Kes sized him up: how he contained his anger and how he breathed it out. "I'll talk to Puck." Before he could thank her, she set the rules. "But if I sense anything getting in the way of your judgment. You're done."

Harrison nodded and headed to the house.

"Harrison."

He stopped and looked back.

"What were you making?"

He looked to the tea towel. "Bread. It helps me think."

IV.

KES WALKED DOWN THE LONG HALLWAY. IT SEEMED TO PASS UNDER THE entire hospital, following the boiler room piping system riveted to the ceiling just above her head. Exactly the sort of place you did not want to be on a fine afternoon like this.

She found the door labelled *Medical Examiner* and knocked on the tiny wire-encased window. A crackle from a speaker beside her sparked to life.

"Yes?"

"Detective Kes Morrison."

The door clicked and slowly swung open. The room had a low ceiling and hummed with fluorescent light. Kes made her way towards the small operating section where an older woman was working at two steel tables. She had an examination lamp pulled low. The woman peered over the top of the lamp, pushed a pair of glasses up on her nose, and pulled down her face mask.

"I'm Connie Hawthorn. Captain Puck said you might be by. Actually, he said I'd be one of your first stops. He thinks very highly of you." The woman had kind eyes, surrounded with well-defined laughter wrinkles, and an oddly soft voice. She appeared better suited to being the matriarch of a large, caring household than working alone in a basement with corpses.

Kes stepped closer to look at the male body and noticed the left eye was missing.

"Was he dead before the shooting?"

"Not much into small talk?"

"Never saw the point."

Connie eyed her curiously. "No, he was killed by the shots. One bullet entered here." She pointed to the man's eye socket. "Likely the one that killed him. Another through the cheekbone. The third, bridge of the nose. I'm told that the female victim who was airlifted to the city has a bullet lodged in her neck. Another in her shoulder. She's in critical condition, not expected to make it."

"His wife?" asked Kes.

"That's your department, dear."

Kes wondered if this could be a family feud. Personal? Domestic? But then why involve the boys at the shooting range?

"He has a needle mark here, on his right upper thigh. I sent samples to toxicology. Preliminary bloodwork has come back positive for ketamine, likely used as a sedative. The half-life indicators suggest it could have been administered three to four days ago, which means it was wearing off at the time of the murder."

Kes looked at the body. It didn't show any signs of bruising or struggle. "Was there something else used?"

"Tox report is negative, but I would suspect a paralytic. Maybe Rohypnol. It's virtually undetectable after three to four hours."

"A date rape drug. Injected. Don't see that often." Kes said.

"Not easy to get, either. Dark web or street. And difficult to get the dose right so that it incapacitates but doesn't kill, and leaves the victim conscious and aware."

"The victims knew what was coming?"

"Yes, I believe they were alert when they were shot."

"He wanted them to suffer." Kes examined the ligature marks around the neck and wrists.

"Hog-tied." Connie pointed to the cord on a side table. "Rope from any hardware store. Half hitch knot. Right-handed, I would say." She went to a side table where two targets were laid out. Only one had three bull's eyes. *Mac Harrison* was written at the top of the page. "It appears this boy was a better shot than the other."

Poor kid. Kes looked back at the body. "Clothing?"

"He had been stripped." Connie returned to the corpse. "Thus far, I haven't found any fingerprints, saliva, or stray hairs. Nothing under his nails. I've swabbed for DNA, but I'm doubtful there'll be any from the killer. They were careful."

"Age?"

"Mid-sixties would be my guess. But he's in good shape."

Kes studied the man's hands. Working hands. Tanned arms. She looked back at the shattered face. *Who are you?*

"I've sent in his prints; hopefully you'll get some answers in the next couple of days if he's in the database."

Kes leaned in to examine the needle mark. "At this point we're the only ones, apart from those on the scene, who know the victims were alive before they were shot, correct?"

"For now, but it will get out. People were there and they'll be talking. It doesn't take long for gossip to make the rounds in a small town." Connie looked to Kes, sensing her concern. "You don't want the boys to know."

Kes looked to the wounds. "How will they live with that?"

"Our job is to unearth the truth, Detective. We serve the victim."

She was right, but Kes's idea of justice and truth had warped long ago. It didn't seem the answer was that simple anymore.

"Let me know if you find anything else."

"The only other thing is this." Connie picked up a metal bowl. At the bottom was a flattened bullet tip. "Not typical for a shooting competition, in my experience." She nodded to a back wall covered in marksman certificates.

"Hollow-point?"

"All three."

"That explains no exit wounds," Kes said.

"Someone wanted maximum internal damage." Connie slipped the bullets into a clear evidence bag and handed it over.

Kes pulled out her phone and took several photos of the man's face. "Thanks for getting on this so quickly."

"Nice diversion from your run-of-the-mill heart attacks," Connie joked. "Good luck," she called after Kes in that soft voice that sounded like a mother's. "Stay safe."

Kes sat in her car in the hospital parking lot jotting down notes. The start of her to-do list for when the world opened up again on Monday. Lists gave her something to follow. A trail. She loved collecting details. This was where the answers were hidden. Disconnected and arbitrary facts would eventually build and rearrange themselves into pieces that fit together. She looked out the windshield.

In another month or so, this place would be slammed with tourists looking for "authentic" Atlantic experiences, lobster dinners and whale-watching tours. Murders didn't bode well for tourist towns. There would be pressure to solve this case, and quickly. Her phone beeped.

"Morris."

"Brownley here."

"What have you got?"

"I found Chester."

"Chester?"

"My partner. We did a chainsaw test. The blade went through the straw no problem but clogged quickly, and now I'm covered in dust and hay. This couldn't have been done on-site without leaving a mess."

Kes flipped over a new page in her notebook as Brownley continued.

"And the straw plug that came out was shaved smaller than the opening because of the width of the blade, so it didn't fit tight. To make it tight it had to be cut from another bale. Chester thinks a carving saw might have been used. Longer blade and finer cut. It would have taken time to carve the hole, fit the bodies, shore up the bales, stitch it back together. A lot of time."

"How long?"

"Days. The bales and plugs had to be prepared beforehand."

Kes made a note. *Somewhere private. Someone with tools and skill.*

"Good job. Chester, too. See you in an hour and a half at the station."

"Yes, ma'—"

Kes hung up. Her fingers touched the pill bottle. It was only four thirty; she should wait another hour. She took the pill. There was still a meeting to get through.

She revved the engine and rolled down her window. Warm spring air wafted in. She reviewed the list of what she now knew and the longer list of what she didn't.

Pulling out of the hospital lot, her mind trying to link the pieces, she nearly cut off an ambulance racing towards Emerg and slammed on her brakes.

V.

ON HER DRIVE BACK INTO TOWN, FAT FREDDY'S DROP PLAYED LOUDLY. The band always made Kes feel good, syncing her heart to its soulful beat. She turned up the hill past the Historic District and pulled up to an old brick building overlooking a lake that provided part of the town's water supply. Even the police station was quaint.

It had been at least ten years since she'd been back. A wealthy American tourist had been stabbed on the waterfront and his grieving widow was all over the news. It had looked like a mugging, but Kes knew immediately it was a hit. The wife and her beau were later picked up in Portugal living off a hefty life insurance payout. The last Kes heard, she was still in jail.

The officer at the front desk was young and greeted Kes with the cheeriness of a receptionist, directing her down the hall to the conference room. She noticed that the entrance had been renovated. The designer's directive must have been to "make it friendly" for those coming in to report lost wallets and passports and make parking-ticket complaints. But the aesthetic improvements, Kes noticed, didn't reach beyond the front desk.

The working offices were the same cramped rooms, worn carpets, scuffed linoleum, and beige walls. She glanced towards Captain Puck's office, not really expecting to see him there. The lights were off and the bent venetian blinds were drawn. She remembered he liked to keep tight working hours. In early and out at five.

Kes walked into the small conference room at eighteen-hundred on the nose. Brownley had his back to her and was regaling a younger man, perched on the edge of the table, with an impersonation of her telling him to clear the crime scene while reciting a barrage of things for him do *immediately*. The young man was laughing hard. She had to admit, it was a pretty good impression. And she'd heard her share.

"Not bad, Brownley, but I think my voice is lower."

The younger man jumped and Brownley turned red. They reminded her of little boys, two class clowns caught by the teacher.

Kes took her place at the front of the room. It was tightly crammed with a mishmash of tables and chairs that seemed too small. The younger detective couldn't hold her eyes. He had sandy hair, a scraggly goatee, and was wearing a seventies-style leather coat and a T-shirt printed with binary code and a joke she didn't get.

"You must be Chester?"

"Yes, ma'am."

"Thanks for the chainsaw tests today. Brownley said you thought it might have been a carving saw. Can that be bought at any hardware store?"

Chester sat up straighter. "More of a specialty market. It's higher-powered than consumer-grade, and expensive."

"Who would use a saw like that?"

"Loggers, landscapers, artists..."

"So we can presume the operator had experience with a saw?"

"I would think so."

"How long have you been a detective, Chester?"

"Two years, not quite."

She held his eyes, testing how long it would take him to look away: three seconds. "Brownley."

"Ma'am?" He looked directly at her, prepared to take whatever reprimand was deservedly coming.

"Did you get the membership list for the gun club?"

"They said they'd have it by tomorrow. The event was hosted locally, but there were other clubs' members participating. They need some time to pull it together."

She set her phone on the table. "On here are photos of the deceased male, and I've requested photos of the female to be sent from ICU. I need them printed and circulated for identification."

"Chester's your guy for that," Brownley offered. "He's a whiz with technical. He's always fixing my computer."

Chester shot him a *Don't admit what you can't do* look and Brownley went quiet. "But Brownley's the one for tracking down anything you need."

"Good to know," Kes said. They had each other's backs, which she liked. Chester was like a protective brother, even though he was younger. She looked around the bare room. "We'll need magnetic whiteboards. Let's get the photos up and build it from there."

She looked to her meagre team. "Right now, all we know is that we have a deceased male and a female in critical condition." Kes held up the evidence bag. "And we have this."

Chester stood up to take a closer look "Hollow-points? Those aren't used in competition."

Kes passed the bag over. "So how did they wind up in the weapons? The boys loaded their guns themselves. Who distributed the ammo? Was it a coincidence that a police officer's son was shooting? How were the boys selected to be first on line? Check with the club about that, too. And why these bullets?"

Chester considered. "More damage?"

She felt the surge of energy she got when she was slipping into a case, or maybe it was just the pill kicking in. "And the bales, where did they come from? Who normally supplied the club?" Kes was pleased both detectives were taking notes.

Brownley looked up. "There's something I was wondering about when Chester was sawing through the bales...tractors normally have a hay spear to move them around, but a spike would have pierced the bodies."

"So the bodies were put there after the bales were in position?" Chester offered.

"Maybe." Kes considered the logistics. "The killer would have to be confident he wouldn't be seen." She liked that they were starting to ask their own questions. "What do we know about the murders?"

Chester considered. "They were planned?"

Kes agreed. "Highly organized. Meticulous. No fingerprints. No DNA. High-risk, in public, and there's every indication that the killer wasn't in a hurry."

Brownley pulled a sandwich from his pocket, unwrapped a corner, and took a bite. It looked like baloney and processed cheese. He swallowed, then added, "And he knew about the competition, the workings of the shooting range, how to get in and out...he knew the area."

"Correct." Kes probed deeper. "The victims were naked. Why?"

"Less DNA evidence, more control of the scene." Brownley wiped away a bread crumb.

"Total humiliation," said Chester. "Degradation?"

"Yes, it was personal," said Kes. "So, we start by finding out the identities of the victims and who they were to each other."

Brownley held her gaze. "Do we have a serial killer?"

"I don't know yet. For now, we treat it like any other murder; we do the homework and connect the pieces. The killer wants his work seen. He's not trying to hide what he did. He sent a message, now we figure out what it means. You have my number. We meet back here tomorrow morning at oh-eight-hundred."

The men got up to leave.

"See you tomorrow, boss," Brownley said.

"Kes," she corrected him. "I don't like boss."

"Night, Kes." But she could hear his unease at trying out her first name.

She watched the two officers leave and wondered how long it would take to get them on her side. She figured Brownley was in his early fifties and probably found that hard to admit. Never left town, likely the same friends since high school. Content with what he had.

Chester was harder to figure out. Early thirties, maybe late twenties. She got the sense he was a lot smarter and more obser-vant than he let on. Either he was nervous, or conceding to his superiors. He didn't have confidence in his own ideas yet. She didn't know if either of them was seasoned enough for this case.

Give them time, she told herself, *let them prove themselves one way or the other.* It had been a long day. Her stomach growled. She had forgotten to eat again.

VI.

THE PUB WAS PACKED AND THERE WAS A DISTURBING AMOUNT OF chatter. Kes chose a stool at the end of the bar so she could watch the people in the dining room. A waitress with an air of seniority, who didn't smile, leaned on the bar.

"What can I get ya?"

"Pint of local ale, please."

The woman pushed herself off the wooden counter and went to the taps. She walked with a don't-screw-with-me authority. A younger man leaned over the bar and gave the waitress a kiss on her cheek. She smiled then. Kes watched her beer overflow under the tap.

This was a local's bar. It was darkly lit, but cozy. Side booths and small tables offered a sense of privacy. When she walked in, most had glanced up and registered her as an outsider before looking away.

A man with a striking mop of curly white hair and long sideburns entered, heading directly for the small room behind her that was crammed with VLTs. He had on a heavy cable-knit sweater and rubber boots. She could smell diesel fuel and cigarettes as he passed by. She guessed he was off one of the boats. The waitress set down her beer and a menu. "Kitchen closes in an hour."

Kes took a drink and savoured the cold ale. The head was perfect. The place was packed, and she trusted the food would be good, too. She scoured the menu. Fried fish or red meat? She wanted something greasy and filling. Something to help her sleep. There was a tap on her shoulder, and she turned to see Harrison. He was still wearing the same plaid shirt with traces of flour on the sleeves.

"Hi," he said.

"Hi. You following me?" she half-joked.

"Well, that'd be one way to demonstrate my detective skills." He pointed back over his shoulder. "Here for dinner."

She looked past him to a table near the door where a young boy was eating fish and chips.

"Your son?" The boy looked happy. "You haven't told him yet."

Before Harrison could answer, a wiry squirrel of man with several days' worth of scruff grabbed him by the neck and leaned in. "Hey man, we just got in, heard what happened down at the range..." He was half in the bag.

"Not now, Carp."

"But fuck, it's so fucked up—"

"Not now, I said."

Carp looked to Kes. "Oh, okay, I get it. Good for you, man." He patted Harrison on the back and winked at Kes on his retreat.

Harrison looked embarrassed. "Sorry about that. I saw you here and just wanted to tell you, I remembered something else. When Mac and I arrived at the range, there was a tractor parked at the back of the clubhouse. Had a hydraulic bale-loader attached to the front. Never saw it there before."

"Thanks, we'll follow up on it."

"Okay." Harrison waited an awkward beat. "Enjoy your drink. Let me know if there's anything else I can do."

She appreciated how he wanted to prove his worth to her.

"Harrison, you might be able to help me. Can you take a look at a photo to see if you recognize the deceased? Maybe you've seen him around? Maybe you've crossed paths?"

Harrison tensed up. "You think this was targeted at me?"

"Just ruling out possibilities." Kes brought up the photo on her phone and passed it to him.

"No, I don't know him." He passed the phone back. "Have you asked around in here?"

She smiled. "People are eating, didn't quite seem appropriate."

"There's someone here I think can help." He reached for her phone. She hesitated only a moment before handing it off. It was worth a shot.

Harrison stopped at his son's table first and Mac responded with a disappointed look, before glaring at her. Fair enough, she was intruding on their time. The waitress returned and Kes quickly put in her order, keeping her eye on Harrison.

He headed to the booth where four older men were the midst of a card game. Kes watched the ease of his approach and how warmly he was greeted. Even though he was a police officer, there didn't seem to be a divide between him and his community. Not like in the city. He directed his questions to a man who seemed to hold the room with his presence. Harrison showed him the phone. The fellow's demeanour sobered and he took a long drink of his pint. He said something to the others and they put their cards down.

Kes took a sip of beer. The conversation had turned serious. Harrison shook the man's hand and set down a twenty on the table for the next round.

Harrison returned her phone. "Carl likes to keep track of people. He says it's Brandon Rakes. Lives off Ivy Path down a dirt road back in the woods.

"Did he mention if Mr. Rakes has a wife?"

"Lives alone. He comes in occasionally to the farmers' market to sell maple syrup. Carl thinks he might have been a draft dodger, but that's a common belief here when you don't know where someone came from."

Kes's meal arrived. "You should get back to your son, Harrison. Thanks for your help. Sorry to have interrupted your dinner and apologies to Mac. Hope I didn't ruin your night."

"Dessert will help." He turned to see Carp leaning sloppily into Mac, who looked like he was on the verge of tears. He met his father's eyes and Harrison saw his son's panic and confusion. Harrison charged towards them. "Carp! Get the fuck away from him."

"I was just asking him about what happened and did he see the bodies..."

Mac looked to his father for the truth and, seeing the answer, ran for the door.

Harrison shoved Carp, who was already off-balance, sending him onto his ass. "You stupid shit—why can't you keep your mouth shut?" He ran out the door after his son.

Carp clumsily got up, staggering. "What the hell's wrong with him?"

"Get the hell out here, Carp!" the waitress barked. "You're cut off tonight."

"I didn't do anything, Cheryl!"

"You stuck your nose where it didn't belong. Get out!"

Carp knew not to argue and slunk out the back door.

There was nothing Kes could do. Sooner or later, the boy was always going to find out sooner or later, but she understood his father's need to protect him. "I can pay for their meals," she said to the waitress. "Harrison's..."

Cheryl looked at her curiously, like she was insulted. "He'll be back." And headed to another table with a bill.

The pub had quickly returned to normal. Kes tried an onion ring, followed by a spoonful of chowder brimming with fish. It was excellent. Exactly the comfort she needed after a long day.

A man sidled up to her. "Can I buy you a drink?"

Kes eyed him. "Sure," she said. "As long as you don't sit here while I drink it."

Upon entering her modest room at the Jib Motel, Kes immediately turned down the heat. The room was a dreary blue, but it was clean with a decent-sized bed, side table, dresser, and TV.

She loved cheap motels. Their sparseness gave her mind space to rest.

She pulled back the patio-door curtains and took in the view overlooking the harbour. She could see the entire town with its piers jutting into the water, many with fishing boats and draggers tied alongside. The warehouses at dockside were a deep crimson red, and with its candy-coloured houses, white steeples, and glow of street lights, the town looked like a cardboard panorama, the backdrop for a child's railway set. It gave it the appearance of innocence. Yet, here she was.

The motel bed was lumpy and the sheets thin. Kes put the TV on mute. She breathed out and bent to the floor and held the position. She stood, and her fingertips almost brushed the ceiling. She burped and could taste beer. She skipped her sit-ups and slipped between the sheets. The pills were wearing off and she was tired.

A street light outside her window lit the room and Kes thought she should close the blinds, but her body didn't respond. The day's evidence floated through her mind. She had made assumptions about the killer. That he was male. Singular. Her father had taught her to assume nothing. But there was instinct, too, and this murder felt masculine—a shooting range, hollow-point ammo, hog-tied rope...

Her eyes closed and she breathed deeper. The victim was a tall man and fit. It would take strength to subdue and move him. But there had been no indication of a violent struggle. Did the victim know his killer? Or was he surprised or distracted before he could react? And the woman...were they together? One person couldn't control them both. There had to be an accomplice. Two killers? More?

Her heart slowed and she conjured a chainsaw in a man's hands hollowing out a bale of hay. Two different-sized cavities. They would have needed the bodies to confirm the size. She imagined the victims tied up, naked, drugged, and the sound of a chainsaw. In her wake-dream state, Kes sat on a tree stump and wove together the thatched plug. It required patience, as did whittling the sticks to thread through the hay. The preparation site was someplace remote. Inside a barn, a shed, somewhere far enough from civilization that they wouldn't be seen or interrupted. She looked around her and saw only thick woods.

There was an alpha. She sensed someone watching her. Someone else. Someone loyal. Trusted.

As she drifted asleep, she could smell hay.

VII.

KES WOKE TO A FOGGY MORNING. SHE COULD JUST MAKE OUT THE MUTED town through the haze. She padded to the washroom, brushed her teeth, and ran her fingers through her hair. She put on the same clothes as the day before but chose a sharp corduroy jacket that was more masculine. Something she thought made her look authoritative, but approachable. Clothing was a strange language.

Looking out at the harbour, she wondered if she should bring a raincoat, but stuffed her sneakers in her bag instead. Today she'd make time for a long run. She grabbed her notebook and headed for the car.

A seagull had shit on her windshield. She made a mental note to follow up on that car wash Brownley had offered. The road up to the police station had heaved from the spring thaw and she had to keep swerving around potholes. By the time she reached the station, the fog was brightening but the chill remained. She could use a coffee.

As expected, Captain Puck was already there and a pot of coffee was brewing. He might not like working nights, but as she recalled, he was always the first in.

"Kes Morris, good to see you again. Thanks for coming." He pushed a mug towards her. "Two cream, two sugar." He was good like that, remembering little details even after all this time. His hair had greyed, his wrinkles had deepened, and his paunch was a little wider, but he still stood with the same commanding posture.

He'd been captain here for fifteen years. His job seemed comprised of a mixture of public relations and mediation that

entailed maintaining the peace between local residents and ine-
briated visitors; dealing with blocked driveways and noise complaints; and shaking hands at town festivals. He was happily a
small-town captain who enjoyed the quiet days and was easing
towards retirement.

"Sorry I wasn't here yesterday to meet you." He took his
seat and waved her to sit. "I was at the golf course when the call
came in. Opening day, the back nine anyway, and then...well,
then there were meetings and interviews to calm the rumours."

She didn't envy his job; it would bore her to tears, and
she wasn't known for her diplomacy. *Insubordinate, sin-
gle-minded,* and *unwilling to compromise* were the terms more
often attributed to her, which she took as compliments. She
respected Puck's willingness to recognize the limits of his
department and not begrudge her help. He just wanted this
thing solved.

"I've set aside the conference room for you again."

"I was there last night," she said.

"And I'm assigning Brownley and Chester to you."

"Met them. They seem..." She searched for a noncommittal
word. "...eager."

The Captain sipped his coffee and added more sugar.
"Chester's young. Not the best in the field yet, but his work with
computers rivals mine with the nine iron." He smiled at his own
little boastful joke.

"In your opinion then, he's very good," Kes toyed.

"Correct." She could tell he was unsure whether she had just
taken a poke at him. She had.

"And Brownley?"

"Like a dog with a new toy. You just have to introduce him
to it first. They're good detectives, Kes, you'll find that out."

She had a sip of her coffee and took in her surroundings.
In the corner of the office was a spinning wheel. An odd object.

Puck followed her gaze. "A hobby I picked up a few years
back. Spinning wool keeps my blood pressure down." He leaned

back in his chair, a position that signalled he was listening. "So, what do we know thus far?"

"The cause of death—"

Puck raised his hand. "I've read the report, Kes. The medical examiner keeps me abreast of developments in my own community." He said it with a smile, but his eyes said *Tell me what I don't know.*

"We believe the deceased male is Brandon Rakes. Lived alone in the woods. I'll be heading there shortly."

"Rakes? Don't know that name. And the woman?"

"Still unidentified."

"What are we looking at here? Drugs, revenge, domestic?"

"It appears to be personal. Organized." She hesitated, and Puck heard it immediately.

"And *what*?"

"I'm not sure it's a singular killer. We don't have any evidence to support that yet, but this all seems too elaborate for one person to control."

Puck sighed and put down his coffee. "I don't know what this world's coming to when things like this can happen here." He looked to Kes as though he hadn't meant to speak that aloud. "I'm glad you're here. Whatever you need, just ask. Do what you have to do to get the bastards, but keep me updated."

"Yes, sir." Kes stood up.

"Don't forget your coffee." As she picked up her mug, he added, "I heard you were with Harrison last night."

She had forgotten the wildfire of small-town gossip. "He was at the pub with his son. I stopped by to have a bowl of chowder." She didn't know why she found herself offering an explanation.

"They make a good chowder," Puck said. "And they've been doing it for over thirty years. Every day just as good, don't know how they do it."

Kes waited a beat, wondering if the conversation was over, but Puck was watching her as though he had a question. She waited.

"Harrison has asked to join the case."

"I don't think that's a good idea," she said.

"I'll leave that up to you."

Back in her car, Kes took a pill and called Brownley to ask him to follow up on the tractor Harrison had mentioned. He sounded as though she had woken him and she checked her watch. It was an hour before duty call. She heard a woman's voice ask if he wanted eggs. She was pretty sure he muffled the phone then. Kes informed him they had an ID on the deceased and that she was heading to Ivy Path Road to check out Rakes's place. He offered to meet her there, but she preferred to do the first walk-through alone. No distractions. Before he hung up he called her boss, sir, and finally settled on ma'am.

The fog was still wafting over Route 323. The yellow line appeared and disappeared, making it seem alive. Kes almost missed the sign and braked hard to make the turn onto the narrow, gravelled lane. She accelerated and the old Jag slid around the bend, making her smile. The pill had begun to suppress the useless information, allowing her to focus in on the singular: an abandoned osprey nest, a *No Trespassing* sign, a rusted barbed wire fence. She noted every deer path and slowed alongside an old logging road, but it was so overgrown it likely hadn't been used in years. It couldn't be the one Harrison had mentioned.

The fog was heavier in this scrubby brush and the trees were wet with condensation. The wipers swiped intermittently. Kes spotted a dirt path, not much wider than a vehicle, with sodden ruts leading into a tangle of woods. She rolled down her passenger window and the smell of salt fog and spruce wafted in. It looked passable. Carefully, she pulled onto the path.

Hemlock, spruce, and pine blended with the new spring greening of maple and beech trees. Her car bottomed out, scraping a rut, and she swung tight to the higher ground before pulling off into a small, natural clearing perfect for turning

41

around. She stepped out and breathed in the forest. This was a beautiful place. Wild, untamed, and apart. Its stillness calmed her. She looked up the road to the low rise of a hill and headed up on foot.

It felt good to move and she picked up her pace. Later, she'd like to come back and run the trails; she wondered if there were bears in the area. The sky was brightening and the fog dissipating, clinging in low pockets of dark underbrush. She shivered, her coat already damp. She crested the rise and the road ended in a clearing. Directly across from her was a log cabin set back against a copse of sugar maples with thin hoses running between the trunks. This was the right place.

The cabin was meagre. It didn't appear well made and certainly wasn't well kept. There was a burn pile near the middle of the clearing, a stack of rusted metal next to a woodshed, and an outhouse. It was certainly remote. And dead quiet. There was a single, jury-rigged power line snaking through the woods to the road. The wood-stove chimney wasn't smoking.

She headed across the yard and hoped the front door would be unlocked. The ground was uneven and pitted with short stumps and dead branches. She moved carefully over the wet, moss-covered rocks. She didn't want to bust an ankle back here. In the middle of the clearing, she paused at the burn pile and kicked at the cold ashes and charred wood. Nothing unusual.

Kes looked to the house and noticed a single wooden chair propped next to the front door. Rakes was accustomed to being alone. She noted the chopping block and axe nearby and looked back to the road. He would have seen anyone coming in. Probably would have heard a vehicle for miles. She looked to the dense woods ringing the clearing. It seemed impassable. She swiped away a blackfly and took a step forward. A branch snapped loudly underfoot. It sounded almost like a gunshot.

A young deer crashed from the woods behind her and bolted towards the cabin. She watched, amazed at its speed, surefootedness, and graceful bounds. There were still white flecks on its back. She marvelled at the power of its hindquarters. It was dazzling, and Kes felt fortunate to see it.

It leapt, and for a fraction of a second, it seemed to freeze mid-air. She saw the glint of a wire, and the deer's front legs wrenched back, neck outstretched, it crashed chest-first into the ground and he world exploded.

Sound shattered and Kes was hurled backwards. Above her was sky. Fire and debris raining down. The scent of fuel and acrid smoke. She slammed to the ground and the shock reverberated through her chest. Her ears were ringing. Sound pulsed, distant and smothered. Glass was shattering. She tried to sit up, but immediately fell back.

Her face was wet; she touched her cheek and her hand dripped blood. She pressed her palm to the wound to staunch it. She tried to roll on her side. *Get up. Get up*, she told herself, but the searing pain drove her back down.

She looked for the deer and saw it lying on its side. Its eyes open, its neck twisted grotesquely, its speckled back drenched in blood, and she passed out.

VIII.

A HAND TOUCHED HER SHOULDER AND SQUEEZED GENTLY. "DETECTIVE? Kes?"

Someone moved her head. She opened her eyes and saw treetops. The fog had burned off and now it was a clear but windy day. Branches swayed high above. She tried to sit up, but pain seared her chest and ribs, forcing her back down with a groan.

"Better to just stay put. I've put a call in to dispatch. They should be here soon."

Kes focused in on the worried voice and the blur of a man peering down at her. Harrison.

"What are you doing here?"

"After our conversation last night, I thought I'd check this place out for myself. Heard the blast and found you."

She struggled to sit up. Her side stabbed and her eyes watered as she curled forward. Harrison placed a hand on her back to support her. "You should wait to get checked over."

She waved him off and knelt, trying to master the pain, then staggered to her feet and leaned heavily against a tree. Slumped to the left, she found she could almost breathe.

The cabin was mostly gone; just the chimney and partial walls remained standing. Smoke rose from the charred logs.

"Lucky you weren't closer when it went off."

"Why are you here?" she snapped.

She tried to push away the grogginess and pounding in her head. Only Puck and Brownley had known her location. She didn't believe in coincidences. Harrison seemed genuinely concerned, but she had met bad cops before. You never knew who was crooked until it was too late.

"I'm a cop and I had a lead," he said defensively, insulted by her suspicion. "I didn't expect to find you. Or this."

She tried to assess whether he was lying, but her head was throbbing. If it were her kid, she wouldn't wait for answers either.

"I'm sorry," he said. "I should have checked with you first."

"Yes, you should have." Slowly and unsteadily, she moved towards the deer's remains. Each step jolted her side. Harrison kept his distance, following behind.

Kes looked down at the creature. It was a young doe. Its eyes were glassy and blood trickled from its nose. Its neck was broken, and a front leg had been shorn off and was lying ten feet away. A deep line slashed its chest where it struck the wire. "She saved my life."

Kes felt a pang that she didn't feel when she looked at human corpses. She looked away from the doe's broken body and tried to remember the deer leaping. Her eyes followed the thin, twisted, snarled wire at her feet. *Someone with military training?* She stumbled towards the smouldering cabin.

"Shouldn't we wait for backup? Get you checked out?"

"I'm fine." She was off-balance and over-corrected as the ground swayed.

Harrison came abreast of her. "Yeah, you look it. There could be another tripwire, and you're not in any state to be climbing through debris." He stepped in front of her. "With all due respect, you could miss something."

Kes wasn't accustomed to being challenged. But she couldn't ignore the flicker of light in her peripheral vision and the piercing ringing in her ears.

"And there's a deep cut on your cheek," Harrison said. "It needs tending."

She had forgotten that she was bleeding and instinctively reached up to feel it. Hot pain jolted her fingertips.

"I have a kit in my truck, I'll patch it up." Harrison guided her to a stump. "The medics will be here soon. Until then, just take a seat."

She wanted to protest, but her legs were giving out. She didn't like to admit weakness. Sitting, she watched him head to his truck. He was right. The pain was affecting her. She breathed in and out slowly, trying to calm her body. She forced her mind back to the case. Someone had put together an impressive show to destroy what evidence there might have been. They could have torched it with the same result. Maybe they were taunting her. Making sure she knew who was in charge. She let the thoughts tumble until the pain numbed.

Harrison returned with a first aid kit. He found a few stitch plasters and an alcohol swab. "This is going to hurt." He leaned in close and she could smell his sweater. Musk, wood, and damp wool. His breath was shallow and his focus intent. He pinched the edges of the gash together tight. She flinched. He looked to her to see if she was okay.

"I'm good," she lied, swallowing a wave of nausea.

The high-pitched whistle had dulled to a low ebbing churn, and through it she could hear a melodic trill. The birdsong was returning. She looked up to source the sound.

"Chickadee," Harrison said, placing the last of three butter-fly bandages over the cut. "That should hold it for now."

"Thanks." She touched her cheek, trailing her fingers over the long, jagged line. It would scar. "I want to take a look at what's left, give me a hand up."

Harrison packed his kit away instead. "Maybe you should sit tight until the bomb squad arrives."

"They're hours away. The cabin was rigged to blow once. There won't be a second wire. I'm fine." But he didn't seem convinced. She struggled to her feet. "I'm not asking for your permission."

She took a couple of tentative steps towards the ruins, wincing with each movement.

"Wait," Harrison called after her.

Kes's patience was growing thin with him. She turned to tell him to stand down and saw him picking up a couple of stout sticks. *What the hell is he doing?*

"It might help for support," he said, handing her one and keeping the other. "And to poke around with. It's bound to be hot. Keep alert for wires or freshly dug holes, disturbed earth—"

"I know what to look for," Kes said, slowly moving towards the cabin. The stick did help. She was sore, but if she stood straight and didn't put too much weight on her left side, it was bearable.

The ground was littered with glass, shingles, and roof rafters. Beyond a toppled log wall, a dented fridge was on its side, milk and juice spilling out. The power line had been ripped away and was likely still live. Bits of newspaper were stuck in branches. Smouldering clothes were scattered around the periphery. The closer they got to the cabin, the smaller the pieces of debris.

Kes stepped over what had been the front door. Her nose crinkled and she could feel heat underfoot. A kitchen table was on its side. Preserves oozed from shattered jars and sizzled on charred wood.

It had been a one-room cabin. Kes could discern the kitchen area by the cooking wood stove, its front now caved in. Across from it was an overturned single bed, the frame's coiled springs exposed. There were pots and pans, broken plates—none of which matched—and a mug still intact. Rakes had been living sparsely.

Harrison carefully probed the ground in front of him with his stick. "What are we looking for?"

"Something to tell us who Rakes was, and what he had that was worth blowing up."

Kes made her way to the centre of the house, flipping over charred piles as she went, careful not to jostle her side. She tried to piece together the debris field, re-imagining where the items had once been. Near the bed, or perhaps once under it, were two charred books. A large chair had been blown outside. At her feet was a rug that had folded in on itself. She flipped over a metal wash basin, revealing a bar of soap and a razor blade. Something glinted on the edge of the wood stove. She gingerly picked it up.

The object was still warm. Silver. *A chain?* The heat had turned it into a fused, snaking glob. She turned it over to find a small, simple cross attached.

"You have any evidence bags on you?"

"Always." Harrison pulled a stash from his back pocket. Kes dropped the necklace into the bag and went towards the books.

Using her stick, she flipped over a burned cover revealing the title page. A Bible. *Rakes was religious?* Beside it, a larger book was splayed open, face down. She could make out the faint etchings of a globe. An atlas. She tipped it over on its spine and the pages fell open, revealing a hollowed-out space larger than her hand. *A secret stash. Maybe drugs?*

She breathed out, trying to ride the slicing pain as she bent over to pick up the Bible. She fanned the pages and an old black-and-white Polaroid fell out. She caught it mid-fall and winced from the sudden movement.

It was a picture of a man, who may have been a younger Rakes, standing with a team of young boys in uniform. One was holding a soccer ball. A third of the picture had burned away. She set the book and photo on the edge of the overturned table, unable to hold the weight any longer.

"We'll take these and bag the photo."

"Will do." Harrison was beside the chimney, scraping at a small rug that had melted to the floor. "I might have something here." His stick hit metal. He got down on his knees and tore away the carpet, revealing an iron ring set in the floor and two rusted hinges. "Root cellar?"

"Too small for a passageway."

"Vault?" He jimmied the stick into the ring to lever it open.

"Wait. It could be wired."

"Now you're being the cautious one?"

She appreciated his barb.

"I'm sure the initial explosion would have fired any others," he said. "Or we can wait for the bomb squad?"

He was using her words against her. "Open it." She didn't take a step back.

Harrison pressed his cheek to the floor so he could peer under the hatch to check for hidden wires. "It's clear."

"Are you sure?"

He checked again, running his finger along the edges. "Yes."

He pulled it open and they both let out a breath. It was empty. Nothing but a shallow, hand-dug hole, no larger than the dimensions of the hatch.

Harrison seemed disappointed. "That's a lot of effort for something this small. What would you keep in that?"

"What you didn't want found." Kes was looking at the drag marks in the dirt, indicating something had been recently removed.

In the distance they could hear the wail of an ambulance. Kes straightened up. "Cordon it all off before they get here. I assume you have tape in your truck?"

"Yes, ma'am." Harrison stood, brushing off his knees.

Kes surveyed the property. "Do you notice anything strange, Harrison?"

He looked around the ruins. "Besides a blown-up cabin?" He focused and broadened his gaze beyond the crumbled walls. "No vehicle," he said.

"No, there isn't." He had the instincts of a good detective, she thought. But that also meant he knew how to cover his tracks. The ambulance was getting closer, accompanied now by police sirens. "Lock it down."

On his way to the truck, Kes called after him. "When we get out of here, our team meets at the station at eighteen hundred. Don't be late."

She wanted to keep him close.

IX.

KES WAS FEELING BETTER WHEN SHE LEFT THE HOSPITAL, BUT THAT could have been the painkillers they gave her. They had bound her torso—bruising and a cracked rib—checked for concussion, and cleaned and stitched the cut on her check. Nine stitches. She hoped it made her look tough. What was that joke? *You should see the other guy.* She smiled. She was a little stoned.

The doc said she had to give the ribs time to heal. Try not to laugh or cough. Sure thing, doc. She'd have to look up the name of the pain med. It gave her a pleasant warm, light buzz. She felt relaxed, but clear-headed. Everything seemed in sharper detail: the soap dispensers, the red of the exit sign, the sun on the pebbled pavement, the green of her car, the chromed grill, Harrison's blue sweater...

Harrison was waiting outside the hospital. She had forgotten he had offered to drive her car back and handed his truck off to one of the officers on-site. It was the only way she had agreed to go to the hospital at the medics' insistence. No way in hell was she leaving her Jag behind.

"They didn't like my handiwork?" Harrison joked.

"This was just prettier," she said. "You did good. Doc said it stopped a lot of blood loss."

"You're okay?" He checked her eyes for the truth.

"Cracked rib, but I'm good." That was enough about her. "Did you find anything else after?"

"A coach's manual for kids' soccer. It's old, from the 1960s. I handed it over with the other items."

Kes gazed off, watching a stray dog cut across the parking lot and disappear through a gap in the fence.

"It's almost six," Harrison said. "Should I give you a ride to the station?" He tapped his ribs. "You might feel it on the turns and bumps."

She looked at him and saw a tiredness in his eyes. "Don't you have to pick up Mac from school?"

His cheek twitched. *His tell*, she thought.

"Mac's with his mom. We thought he should get out of town for a bit. He can see a specialist there, so...it's better for him."

She could see it wasn't better for Harrison. This was a grieving father. He could never inflict that pain on his son. She remembered how gently he had bandaged her wound and his concern that he was hurting her. He wasn't a killer. She had no doubt he was a good cop, who had followed a lead in the same bullheaded way she would have.

She headed to the passenger side. "Better get moving then, if you don't want to be late on your first day. You're with me, my direction. This is a trial period."

"Understood."

"You can drive this time." She felt light as she eased into the seat. "But then I get the keys back. And don't grind the gears." She rested her head against the window and slipped into the purr of the engine starting.

They pulled into a visitor's space in front of the police station at 6:05, which irritated Kes. She hated being late. Harrison handed her the keys and she struggled to get out of the car. Every movement was excruciating. Harrison offered her a hand, but her glare made him back off. She headed for the door, defying her hurt body. As a runner, she had trained herself to subdue pain, wrap it tighter and tighter in her mind until it was the size of a pebble, but this she couldn't contain.

As she entered, she caught her reflection in the glass door. An ugly yellow was spreading towards her eye. And the bandage made her look like a victim. She pulled off the gauze. The cut was larger and the stitches more noticeable than she had imagined. Harrison stood back and didn't say a word. *Wise man.*

She took a small breath before she stepped into the conference room. The forced smile made her cheek twinge. Brownley and Chester were seated in the front row like perfect students. Harrison joined them.

"Sorry I'm a bit late. Unforeseen circumstances." She propped herself against the desk, knowing her body would rebel against a seated position. They stared at her cheek, but knew better than to ask. "Harrison is joining us. You know each other." The detectives gave him welcoming smiles, but a soft warning in their eyes said this was their turf.

"Sorry about your kid..." Brownley offered quietly.

Harrison shut it down quick, "He'll be all right." Then added, "Thanks."

"Brownley and Chester will get you up to speed on what we know so far." She looked to her detectives to clarify that Harrison wasn't their responsibility. "He'll be working directly under me. Okay...as you've likely heard, we went to what we believe is, or was, Rakes's residence earlier today. If you haven't heard, you can read it in the report later."

Chester piped up. "A friggin' deer tripped the line, really?"

Kes saw a flash of the mutilated deer and pushed it away. She nodded. "Someone was cleaning up. We didn't find any evidence that our female victim lived there." She glanced to the board, where the crime scene photos of Rakes had already been tacked up with magnets. "Any progress on the victim's background?"

Brownley checked his notes. "Nothing yet on Rakes. I showed his picture around and some remembered him from the market but didn't know his name."

"Isn't that unusual for a small town?"

"Not really, there's miles of back roads around here if you want to keep apart and plenty of people who choose to do so."

"He's also a ghost online," Chester added. "No credit cards, no taxes, no bank accounts, no tickets, no driver's license."

"And the female victim?"

"Nothing yet from the city. I've left multiple messages and will follow up in the morning." Brownley jotted down a reminder note.

It irritated her that the city wasn't co-operating swiftly. "Leave another message tonight, give them my name." *That should wake them up.* She had taught and trained half of them and wasn't shy to pull rank. "Harrison, you have the photo?" He rifled through the evidence box and handed her a bag.

Kes studied the photograph. The man, whom she suspected was Rakes, seemed to be in his late twenties. There wasn't a discerning crest on the uniforms, no background that gave a hint as to the location. Just woods and a chain-link fence. Several boys were missing at the edge of frame, where the image had been destroyed. She counted nine. Kes guessed their ages to be between twelve and fourteen. She handed the Polaroid to Harrison.

"How old would you say these lads are? As old as your son?"

"Maybe this one," he said, pointing to the boy closest to the man. "But not the others. Ten to eleven, perhaps? This one maybe even younger." He passed it along to the others.

"Recognize anything or anyone?" she asked. But no one did. Kes pegged it up next to the morgue photos and tapped the image of the man. "Chester, can we confirm this is a younger Rakes?"

"I can try a facial-recognition program, and if that doesn't work I can age him up."

"Let's start there. What else do we have?"

"I followed up with the bales," said Brownley. "The ones you noticed at the entrance came from Paul Winters's farm. It's a dairy operation close to the gun club. Since the big milk producers cut the quotas for small farmers, Winters turned to selling straw and baled hay. The ones you saw at the entrance were his, baled last fall. But the ones that the boys fired at…" He set down photos of the targets. "…were older by the colour and dryness, probably from the previous season, and not from his farm. They're larger and used a different twine. They'd been stored inside. They weren't wet, no mould or rot."

"Kept for the occasion?" Kes shifted on the edge of the table and her side tweaked. Harrison seemed uneasy and she wondered if he could hold his own in the room. "So it's possible this was a long-game plan by someone who knew the area."

Brownley understood immediately. "You think someone from around here did this?"

Kes recounted the facts. "At least one of our victims is local. The killer knew about the shooting competition…"

"…and where Rakes lived," said Harrison, finishing her line of thought. She appreciated that he wasn't going to just sit back and observe. The men pondered the implications.

"Anything else?

Chester raised his hand, which amused her. "I checked on the shooting order. It was a random draw. Anyone could have been at the line." He said this directly to Harrison, whose shoulders lowered in relief. He wasn't the target.

The door flung open and Captain Puck entered. He was wearing golf clothes and looked windswept. He stopped when he saw Kes's face. "Goddamn it. You all right, Detective?"

"I'm fine." She respected that he had come back after hours to check in on them. Had to see for himself. "I've asked Harrison to join us for a bit. Probationary, of course."

"Good," Puck replied, still evaluating her injuries. He had noticed the twinge of her eye when she straightened to answer him, but standing before him now, her body betrayed nothing. "I understand you passed your detective's exam with high honours." Brownley and Chester glanced Harrison's way. "This is the team to train you up."

"Thank you, sir." Kes heard *I will not disappoint you.*

"Keep me apprised," Puck said to Kes. "I don't like hearing about one of my detectives almost being blown up. Make sure you take the evening off. That's an order."

"Yes, sir." She could see him questioning if he was being mocked. She knew she was hard to read. She preferred it that way. "Thank you for checking in." He nodded and she knew he understood she was being sincere.

She turned back to her team. "Tomorrow we should be getting details about the explosives and how the cabin was rigged. We're missing the *why*. Why go to all this effort to kill? There are easier ways. This was a performance."

She felt something twitch under her skin, a gnawing that was deep and brutal. She pushed it away. Her legs were trembling and soon she wouldn't be able to hide the pain. The meds were wearing off.

"That's enough for today. Get some sleep; I need you sharp tomorrow. Whomever we're dealing with is in control at the moment—let's change that." She got up, swallowing a groan. "I'll see you in the morning."

Chester looked to Brownley in a silent exchange of respect. She was tough. Maybe tougher than them.

As she passed Harrison he nodded his thanks, but she pretended not to see.

Kes took a moment to watch a red-tailed hawk circle slowly overhead, then started up her car. She drove with one hand, no longer having the mental stamina to overcome the pain. Even through her exhaustion, she noticed how pretty the drive was along the harbour road leading to town.

She spotted a fish and chip truck with a few customers milling about and pulled in. She ordered takeout, made a stop at the liquor store for a couple of beers, and headed to the dock. She sat on a picnic table at the end of the pier to eat her dinner and let the harbour's beauty wash away the day. The beer was cold and the setting sun warm. She tossed some fries to the seagulls and watched them reel in the sky, snatching morsels from each others' beaks.

This is the good, she reminded herself. When the case flickered in her mind, she forced it away. *Not now.* Now was her time to sit with herself.

X.

Someone high up in the window of a concrete tower was watching her, but she couldn't see their face. She stepped forward and the building imploded. Floor after floor collapsed and a white cloud of dust engulfed her. *Run*, she told herself. *Run!* But she stood still. Her ears were ringing and the ringing became louder, more rhythmic and insistent.

Kes snapped awake, recognizing the sound, and reached for her cellphone, which caused her to curl up in pain. She answered through clenched teeth: "Morris."

"Puck here. There's been another murder." His words were tight and brittle.

"Where?" She reached for her notebook and scribbled down the directions. "I'll be right there. Get the team to meet me."

She hung up and rolled off the bed, careful not to put pressure on her side. She pulled on a loose pair of slacks and eased a clean shirt over her tender ribs. She couldn't raise her arms high enough to pull her hair back into a ponytail so she left it loose. A quick brush of her teeth and she was ready. The woman looking back at her in the mirror made her pause.

Her eyes were pinpoint sharp and her forehead creased with the strain of pain. The bruise had widened into a mottled purple-black and sickly yellow around the stitches and underneath her left eye. She took one of her pills and one of the pain meds. She checked the time: 6:30 A.M. It was still dark.

Kes arrived at the wharf and spotted Harrison's truck. The sky was blueing to twilight and the street lights were still on. The morning was chilly so she grabbed her jacket from the trunk, but didn't bother to zip it up. She flashed her badge and crossed the barricade tape and headed down the timber wharf to a fishing boat idling at the end of the pier.

On-board, a huge man wearing a tattered sweater full of holes was holding the bow of the boat close to the dock. "You the detective?" he asked.

"Yes, Detective Kes Morris."

He held out a hand to help her aboard. "They said it would be easy to recognize ya." She didn't ask him to elaborate.

"Helluva a way to start the morning," he said as she climbed down the pier's iron rungs. She hesitated to calculate the step between the wharf and the gunwale, the boat's motion, and the gap between. "Don't think, just step."

She took his hand and trusted. She found her footing quickly on deck and nodded to Brownley, Chester, and Harrison, who were seated along the gunwale.

"Cast off, Cecil," barked the boat's captain from the wheelhouse. The deckhand flipped the bowline to the wharf and planted himself on the foredeck with his legs parted. He lit a cigarette as the boat's engine revved, pushing them out into the harbour. Cecil barely rocked. Kes lost her balance and grabbed the rail to steady herself. She made her way to her team, still trying to find her legs, and sat heavily beside them. She couldn't hide the wince that jolted her side. The diesel fumes reminded her of the fishing trip she'd made with her father when she was ten. He never put a line in and was seasick the entire time, but he had insisted on taking her out. He wanted her to know what the sea felt like. He didn't want her to be afraid of it.

"What do we know?" she said.

Brownley shouted over the engine's din. "He found it." He nodded towards the captain. "Captain Phil. They've been out lobster fishing. Every few days, they bring their catch in here and dump them in the lobster cars—"

"Cars?"

He pointed to the buoys dotting the harbour. "Pens, cages for live holding. They arrived early this morning to dump their catch."

The captain pulled the throttle back and slipped the boat into reverse, expertly nudging the vessel broadside against a partly submerged holding tank. Cecil jumped down from the bow onto the wire mesh roof and tied off the boat.

Captain Phil turned to the detectives. "It's sick, I tell you. I've seen a lot at sea. But this..."

He switched on a row of lights on the masthead and panned them to the cage. Kes and her team headed to the port side as Cecil walked across the lobster car, creating the illusion that he was walking on water. He stopped and looked back to his captain.

"Open it."

"Fuck me," Cecil breathed, gathering his courage, and lifted the lid.

Kes could see hundreds of lobsters, their claws banded, packed deep in the holding tank. They were churning, writhing, and climbing over each other. Cecil got down on his knees and pulled away several lobsters from the centre of the cage, revealing the crown of a human head.

"Can we get him out of there?" Kes asked.

Cecil took a step back. "I'm not doing that by myself!"

"Chester. Harrison." They didn't hesitate. She noticed that both were wearing their work shoes. None of her team had thought to bring rubber boots. They sloshed onto the top of the pen.

Kes looked to Captain Phil. "Do you have a tarp?"

"Under the aft seat."

Brownley stood up. "I'll get it." She tried to help him spread it out on the deck, but her injury constricted her.

"I've got it." Brownley gently took her end of the tarp. She was being more of a hindrance than a help. She went back to port side to watch the men's progress. They were scooping lobsters out of the pen and onto the top of the car. The creatures with banded claws scrabbled over the mesh towards the edge. Cecil was grabbing them and pulling them back. A man's head and shoulders emerged.

"Fuck!" Harrison jumped back, clutching his hand.

Cecil peered into the cage and called back to the boat. "Some of 'em have been un-banded!"

"Aww for shit's sake." Captain Phil pulled himself over the gunwale. For a big man, he was spry. He strode to the opening. "If you see a feller without elastics, grab him and toss him."

Chester tossed a lobster over the side.

"Not into the drink, onto the boat! Fuck sakes almighty. We band every damned one of them. Cecil, corral the ones with rubbers—don't let 'em get back in the water or they're good as dead." Cecil scrambled to herd the escaping lobsters.

"Catch," he said to Brownley, tossing a two-pounder his way before he could object. Brownley caught it by the tail and swung it away from his body to avoid the grasping claws.

The captain took command of Harrison and Chester. "If you get under his arms, you can pull him out and we can be done with this."

Kes suppressed a small tweak of irritation that someone else was directing her team, but he wasn't wrong, and she knew that on a boat, the captain was in charge. Chester and Harrison knelt down and got on either side of the body.

"Watch out for the claws," Harrison said. "There's one by your left hand." Chester pulled back quickly and re-positioned. "Ready? One, two, three."

They heaved and dragged the body out of the cage. Chester lost his footing and fell backwards with the corpse. "Jesus Christ!"

He rolled and squirmed away. A lobster had grabbed his coat sleeve and Chester swatted at it wildly. Harrison reached over and yanked it off. They looked to Kes. What a shit show.

"Let's get him up here," she said.

Brownley grabbed the corpse under the arms as Harrison and Chester hoisted him over the gunwale, while Cecil and Captain Phil tossed lobsters back into the car.

The body slid belly first onto the deck and the waiting tarp. Brownley helped Chester and Harrison climb aboard. They stood, sodden and shivering, looking down at the corpse. Blood trickled from a cut on Harrison's finger.

Brownley rolled the body over. The man was wearing a diving mask with a snorkel attached.

"He was put in alive." Chester said what they were all thinking.

Kes took a photo with her phone and pulled off the mask and placed it beside the man's chest. He was an older man, late sixties perhaps. His face seeped blood from where lobsters had nipped at him. He had long, greyish hair tied in a thin pony-tail and was wearing a black suit and tie, like he was dressed for a wedding, or more likely a funeral. She took several more pictures.

"Dammit!" the captain shouted. They turned to see a lobster hanging from his finger. He shook it off into the pen and Cecil laughed. "Good thing it was the pincer not the crusher, would have taken 'er right off."

"Shut 'er, Cecil." He looked down into the pen. "What are we going to do with these? Whose gonna eat them now?"

Kes looked back to the dead man. Lobsters were latched onto the body, between his legs, on his belly; some fingers were bent and snapped. She pulled the tarp over him.

XI.

THE TIDE WAS LOWER AND THE SKY BRIGHTER. AS THEY APPROACHED the dock, Kes could see Captain Puck and a waiting ambulance. Connie was suiting up near the medical examiner's van. Farther beyond, a small crowd had gathered by the barricade and a couple of officers were keeping watch. There was also a cameraman and a reporter, mic in hand. The boat bumped the end of the wharf and the captain flung a line up onto the deck.

"Tie that off," Captain Phil ordered the paramedic standing at the edge of the pier.

"I don't know how—"

"You know how to tie your shoelaces, don't you?" He headed back to the wheelhouse to cut the engine.

Cecil flung another line from the bow and scurried up the rungs to secure it, which seemed to take him mere seconds to tether and coil. Then he grabbed the bowline from the medic who was fumbling it into a tangled mess.

A stretcher was lowered into the boat and Chester and Harrison helped them load the body, lobsters still attached, and strap it tight. Captain Phil joined Kes to watch them hoist it up.

"That's no way to die," he said. "No dignity in that."

You're right about that, Kes thought. "How do you think they got the body in there?"

"Crammed it in, I'd say. Just needed him on his knees."

She noted the captain's arthritic hands, which were double the size of hers. He looked like the kind of man who'd win in a brawl, but his eyes were soft and contemplative, belying his gruffness. She'd like to have a beer with him.

"Thanks." She shook his hand. It was a strong grip that smothered hers. She had to tense her side to absorb the pain of the movement.

"Come by my office anytime." He grinned, gesturing to the boat. "Good luck finding the bastard who did this."

She awkwardly climbed the ladder using only one hand, the other bracing her side, and was helped to the top by Captain Puck. Cecil waved a friendly goodbye as he lit another cigarette.

"Well?" asked Puck.

"It's connected, and now I'm certain it's more than one killer."

Puck sighed. Another day of calming politicians and civilians lay ahead. "I'll call Susan to put on coffee. See you back at the office."

Puck walked to the boat with his phone to his ear. He greeted Cecil and shook his hand. *A natural politician*, she thought.

She gathered her team around her. The sun was poking above the buildings and everything was beginning to take on its festive colours like nothing had happened.

Brownley quietly said, "It's the same guy, isn't it?"

"Guys, I'd say." She looked to Harrison and Chester. "It took both of you to get the body out. This couldn't have been done alone. We're dealing with serial killers."

"Random?" asked Chester.

Kes shook her head, considering the possibility. "This seems more personal. More targeted. The killings aren't uniform and there isn't an apparent signature."

"Both are doing the killing?" Harrison asked.

"I don't know yet. We know the killers are strong, perhaps athletic, or at least fit..."

"Familiar with lobster cars," Brownley added.

"And they're hunting in the same ground. Bringing the bodies to this town." Kes looked to her men. Chester was shivering. All were wet.

"Go get changed, warmed up, have some breakfast, and take care of that cut." She nodded to Harrison's nicked hand. "I'll see you back at the office in an hour."

On the way to her car Kes stopped to check in with Connie, who was donning her gloves and surgical mask.

"Hold him there a moment," Connie called to the paramedics. "I want to take a look before you load him." She turned to Kes. "Nothing like an autopsy before morning coffee."

Kes smiled softly; she liked this woman. "Could you check for needle marks and test for the drugs used in the shooting-range murders?"

Connie's eyes narrowed, understanding the implication.

"I need to know if he was alive before he was put in the pen. If he's the around the same age as the other victim."

"I know how to do my job, Kes."

"Sorry. I know you do, Connie. They're more questions that I'm asking myself."

Connie looked to the town ringing the harbour. "I wonder how they managed to do this with all these houses full of notoriously prying eyes?"

Kes staved off a small shiver. She couldn't tell if it was the drug or the morning's chill. "Most were looking inward, I guess."

"I'll call you when I have something."

Kes headed for her car and called back: "Watch out for the lobsters!" Connie lifted the sheet on the body and took a step back. Kes almost laughed. The pills were finally kicking in.

As she approached the caution tape, the reporter raised her mic. "Detective Morris. Can you tell us what you found out there?"

Kes wondered how the reporter knew her name. "I found out that a lobster has two distinct claws and the crusher is more dangerous than the pincer."

She brushed past the assembled onlookers.

The reporter called after her. "Detective, they don't call you in unless it's a major crime. Is this connected to the killing at the shooting range?"

Kes kept walking. She had work to do.

XII.

Sunlight shone on the floor tiles. Kes, sitting on the edge of the conference table, swung her legs in the light. It pulsed and shimmered through the trees outside. She was mesmerized by its movement. Everything moved about, didn't it? Just when you thought you could grasp it, it slipped away. Like this case, moving so fast. This wasn't the end of it. Not yet. She took a sip of black coffee and looked up. She was surprised to see everyone sitting in their chairs facing her. The pills were stronger than she thought. Puck was leaning against the back wall.

"Sorry. Just thinking." She smiled tiredly. "Chester, I'll need you to print photos of our latest victim." She pulled out her phone and sent him the images. His phone dinged. She looked to the sparse whiteboard displaying only one victim. "Brownley, where's the photo of the woman I asked for?"

"There's nothing in my box. I've called the hospital again."

"Captain, will you call and get them to send a bloody photo of the victim? And her fingerprints? You'd think that would be a simple request."

Puck pulled out his phone and stepped outside. Kes pushed down her anger. She hated incompetence.

"We have three crime scenes now." She wrote on the board *Gun Range, Cabin, Lobster Car*. "And there have to be ancillary sites where the actual preparation took place. What do we have so far? Let's start with the gun club. Reports: Brownley."

"I have a list of members and participants. All are known by the organizers. No one stands out. The names have been run. No flags raised."

"Chester?"

"Called around to see if anyone was missing a new tractor. Dispatch took a call about an hour ago from a Harold Braun, eighty years old. He was away for the weekend and found his missing when he got home."

"Sons?"

"One's a banker and the other's a veterinarian. Both out of province." Chester checked his notes. "No fingerprints on the tractor apart from Harold's."

"Head to the farm later and take a look around for anything that might be helpful. Tire tracks, cigarette butts...maybe there's a vacant barn or shed on the property where the bales were prepped."

Harrison raised a hand.

"You can just speak." It sounded curt. She couldn't hold back the edginess that was creeping in behind the pills.

"I remembered something else about the morning of the competition," he said. "There were three judges and normally there's only two. Judges are sent in from another club to mitigate favouritism."

She was feeling the low growl of impatience. *Why didn't they already know this?* "Who were the judges?" She turned to Brownley.

He checked the list. "There are only two recorded."

"Follow up on that." She looked to Harrison. "Did you get a look at him?"

"He had a ballcap pulled low. I only saw him from behind. We were already on the line."

"Did he pass out the ammo?"

"I was focusing on Mac, I don't know."

She had to remind herself that he was a victim that day, a civilian out with his son, not a cop. She wouldn't have noticed either.

"So we have someone possibly at the starting line who didn't belong there." Early in her career, she had caught a case where the killer was a paramedic who'd rushed in to treat his own victims. Hiding in plain sight. "He might have been there to watch his own handiwork." She looked to Brownley. "Talk to the other judges; interview everyone who was there, see what they remember."

She knew she was speaking too quickly, unable to slow her thoughts. "Chester, do we have any more on Rakes?"

"Brandon Rakes doesn't exist. At least not on the internet. I ran every face-recognition and aging program available on the photos. The state of the corpse and the quality of the photo make it more difficult, but I'd say we have a seventy-percent match between the victim and the man in the Polaroid. If I have more time and do some reconstruction, I might get it higher. There's a shadow obscuring part of his face."

Kes was feeling the prickle of too many unknowns. "Track down soccer teams and schools in the county dating back thirty to forty years; maybe we can match him or the kids that way." She looked at the photo on the whiteboard. "Maybe he changed his name? Try names close to Brandon Rakes. Rake Brandon. Rick Brandon. Richard. People often stick close to what they know."

"I'll run it through again this afternoon." Chester scribbled on his pad.

"And the cabin?" she asked.

Brownley spoke up: "Nothing further was found on the premises. There's no chance of prints. The explosives were garden variety. Fertilizer and propane. The tripwire sparked it."

"And our lobster man..." Kes sighed. *Another unknown.* "Start tracking who he is."

Puck returned. Kes looked to him expectantly, but frowned when she saw the tightness of his mouth. "What?"

"They've lost her. The second victim."

"The woman in a coma?"

"Late last night. Tubes unplugged and her bed empty."

"What, she walked out?"

"Doesn't look that way. They say she couldn't have regained consciousness. She was heavily sedated."

"For shit's sake!" She couldn't restrain herself. "How do you lose a comatose victim?"

"There were a couple of large drunk-and-disorderlies in progress downtown, university parties. All active police were directed to the scenes, including the officer stationed with our victim."

Kes didn't want to hear excuses. "I want everyone on that floor interviewed, surveillance checked, every closet and bathroom searched. If the killers were finishing the job, then she's still there...and when they find her, tell them to take a damn photo and fingerprints!"

The room was silent. "It's underway, Kes." Puck's eyes warned her to compose herself.

She took a deep breath and held the hot twinge of pain in her ribs. She reined in her racing mind. "How did the killer know she was there? The media weren't informed about a second victim, but the killers knew she was still alive. How?"

"They were watching," Harrison said. "At least one of them was still at the shooting range."

She honed in on Harrison again. He had known the woman was still alive. He had found the first victims. He was at the cabin when it exploded and with them again this morning. What did she really know about him? He held her gaze. She looked deep and saw only openness and honesty. She was off her stride. The pain, the pills, the muddled evidence. *Follow the trail,* her father would say. *Follow it until you can smell it.*

"Start chasing it down," she said to her team.

Puck stayed behind a moment longer. "Pace yourself, Detective," he counselled, and followed his men out.

"Sir." Puck turned around. Kes chose her words carefully. "How much authority do I have to find them?"

His eyes hardened. "Do what you have to do to end this."

XIII.

The police station bathroom was cramped. Puck's secretary, Susan, had tried to add a feminine touch with a floral soap dispenser. On the back of the toilet was an aerosol air freshener and a sign posted: *If you sprinkle when you tinkle, be a sweetie wipe the seatie.*

Kes washed her face and ran her fingers through her hair. Puck was right. She was taking this personally. She had trained herself not to show anger, but she had just revealed her frustration to the whole team. She tried to blame the pain, the exhaustion, the disorientation of being in a new place alone, again. She looked herself in the eyes and said, "Liar."

She knew her process. She knew the itch under her skin. The cold hardness creeping in. She was pulling the killer's skin on too fast. She was beginning to feel the detachment and calculation, the sadistic pleasure. No, not pleasure. This wasn't sexual. *Control?* It was always about control. *Vengeance?* Maybe that was the taste on her tongue. *Brutal, righteous retribution.* But what was the crime? Something wild flickered across her heart. She looked into her eyes.

"What was their crime?" she asked. But only her constricted pupils stared back.

She repeated Puck's words: "Pace yourself." Keep the emotion away. Whoever this was, they were her prey. She had to find the balance between seeing through their eyes and holding onto herself. She tilted her head, the bruise under her eye had turned a darker shade. Her ribs felt tight. She slipped a finger under the tensor binding and pulled it away from her side for a moment of relief. She took a deep breath. *One step at a time.*

In the station, her team was squirrelled away at their desks, manning phones and computers. Susan, who dressed like a den mother right down to her soft pastel cardigan, smiled as she passed Kes in the hall carrying a cup of coffee to Puck's office. At the front desk, a couple of officers were filling out forms for a fender bender. Harrison went up to greet them and they ribbed him for "crossing over to the other side." The place seemed almost jovial. She noticed Susan discreetly set down a muffin next to Brownley's computer. When he reached for it, he squeezed her hand. This was a family.

"Harrison, let's go," she said.

She had acquiesced when Harrison suggested coffee. She was still feeling the chill of the morning. The Quayside Café was warm and decorated in a nautical theme. An older woman with a purple stripe in her white hair took their order. Two lattes to go. The woman's gaze lingered on Kes's stitched cheek and black eye.

While the coffee machine whined, Kes flipped through the photos on her phone of the latest victim. She expanded the image to magnify his face. Eyes closed. Wet hair. Marks around his eyes where the scuba mask had left its imprint. The waitress set a latte with a foam heart beside her.

"Jeezus," said the waitress. "What happened to Doc? Is he okay?" Kes flipped her phone over. "I'm sorry, I didn't mean to snoop. It was right there."

"You know this man?" She glanced to Harrison, who took out his notepad.

"Not well. Doc Wilson. Black coffee. Chocolate chip cookie. No tip. He'd sometimes come in here and leaf through his stamp-collecting books. I told him my grandson was a stamp collector, too. Got into it when he was at home with a busted leg. He liked the history of it. *Philatelist*, Doc corrected me." She gave a grin that showed badly crooked teeth. "Big on himself, that way."

"Doc Wilson. What kind of doctor?"

"None that I know of. It's just what people called him."

"Do you know where he lives?" Harrison asked.

"The end of Hobson Road. Old place on the hill."

"I know it," Harrison said.

Kes set her money on the counter, grabbed the latte, and looked to Harrison. It was time to go.

"Can I take a rain check on mine?" He put a fiver on the counter.

"Sure," she said. "You won't tell him I said anything, will you?"

"You don't have to worry about that," Harrison said.

Kes grabbed an extra sugar and a stir stick.

"Miss." The waitress leaned over the counter and smiled at Harrison, who was waiting at the door. She handed Kes the café's business card and quietly said, "If you need anything..." She looked to Kes's cut. "There's people who can help you."

Kes touched her cheek. "Oh no. No, I'm fine. Work injury." She handed the card back.

"Keep it anyway," the waitress said. "In case."

"It's just two blocks up the hill," Harrison said. They'd taken his truck. He'd used the rationale that the truck might be more useful if they had to go off-road, but they both knew it was about giving her body more time to heal.

They passed old wooden homes built atop steep stone foundations that clung to the side of the hill. Most had ornate scrollwork around windows and doors that were meticulously painted with agreeable combinations of complimentary colours. This was a wealthy neighbourhood.

They turned onto Hobson and the road levelled out. A few older residents puttered around their front lawns, preparing flower beds for planting. Kes felt like she had stepped back into the last century, when the town was booming with seafaring ventures. They passed a monument to Norwegian sailors and just beyond that at the end of the street, tucked back and forgotten, was the victim's house poking out from a row of scrubby trees. It showed the neglect of time.

Kes sent Chester a text for information on the address.

"Are we going in?" Harrison eyed the path. "We know what happened last time you tried entering a house."

Kes considered the risk. She looked to the elderly couple across the street clearing their lawn of winter debris. "I think they've already announced themselves and now they're focusing tighter."

Her phone chimed. *Sole owner. Occupant. Name on deed: Arnold Wilson.*

"Should we call the captain and cover our bases?"

"The captain's aware of how I work." She stepped out of the truck.

The lawn had been recently mowed, making it easy to see any tripwires or booby traps. They slowly advanced. Kes headed up the wooden stairs. Harrison signalled for her to wait and Kes paused on the landing. He pointed to his ear and then to the house. He drew his weapon. Kes could hear a scratching sound coming from inside. She tucked back and braced herself against the wall. The front door was slightly ajar. Slowly, she pushed it open, looking for wires as she did so.

A large tabby cat sprang out and darted into the bush. Kes's heart jumped and adrenaline surged, but she didn't twitch. Harrison kept his weapon trained on the entry. Kes gently pushed it open until they were looking down a short hallway lined with stacks of newspapers and magazines. A pungent, overpowering smell emanated from the house. A mix of cat piss and sour, stagnant air.

They carried on down the hall that led to the kitchen, where more piles were heaped against the walls like they were supporting the building, blocking the only window in the small room. The cupboard doors were open and the drawers had been rummaged.

"We aren't the first ones here," she said.

"God, that smell. I can taste it." Harrison breathed through his mouth. "Do you think he was using these like sandbags? Like a bunker?"

"Or he was just a hoarder."

Harrison glanced into the other main floor rooms. "It's clear." He holstered his weapon. They pulled on latex gloves. "This place is probably crawling with fleas."

"I'll take down, you take up," Kes said.

She looked around the kitchen. One chair, two mugs, two mismatched plates, a radio, a cat bowl. She opened the fridge. Bread, butter, and cheese. She couldn't discern any order in the vast array of outdated magazines and papers.

She headed into the living room. It was darkly shrouded by heavy curtains. The walls were bare. No personal pictures. Nothing revealing who Doc Wilson was. There was a TV, a chair with the imprint of a person who had sat there hour after hour, and a couch covered in cat hair. She went to the bookshelf and flipped through the books to see if there was anything hidden between the pages, but found nothing.

Kes could hear Harrison's footsteps a floor above. She went back to the stairs. Something was off. She re-entered the kitchen and tried to see past the stacks of clutter. She looked up to the ceiling and the windowless back wall. This room's footprint was smaller than the other side. She returned to the living room. She ran her hands over the panels and bookcases along the staircase wall. A panel creaked loose. She pushed harder, and a hidden door released.

She stooped to enter. The room was dark, and she felt the wall for a light switch. The space illuminated, revealing a heavy wooden table with lamps and magnifying glasses placed in front of a leather chair. The far wall held rows of books dedicated to stamp collecting.

"I found your treasure," she said.

On the floor, beneath empty shelves, were collectors' albums that had been placed on their spines in rows. Paint had been poured over the books. Green, red, and gold. The paint was still wet. The gallon tins had been tossed aside.

Harrison descended. "I'm under the stairs," she hollered. "Through the living room."

She found a pen on the desk and used it to open one of the sodden books. She skimmed away the paint to reveal old stamps, dissolving and curling in the wet. She could make out a three-masted schooner, postmarked 1870.

Harrison came up behind her. "What a mess," he said.

"Looks like they wanted to destroy something he loved." She looked back at the chair. "And they would have wanted him to see it happening. This is where it started." *How long were you here?* she wondered. "Get a team to come in and dust. Doubtful they'll find anything, but let's go through the motions."

"I found this upstairs," he said, and held up an evidence bag. Inside was a small silver cross and chain. "It was pinned with a tack at the head of the landing. I think it was meant to be found."

Kes took the bag and went to the other side of the desk and sat in the chair. She could see the full scale of the collection's destruction: A life's work desecrated. Panes of stamps shredded. Drawers open, the contents strewn on the floor. Loupes, magnifying glasses, empty sleeves and glassine envelopes, and the long row of albums bleeding paint.

She looked at the cross. It was identical to the one found in the cabin. She drew it out of the bag and ran the chain between her fingers.

It was tarnished and cheap.

XI.

KES STARED AT DOC'S AND RAKE'S PICTURES ON THE WHITEBOARD. SHE had mounted the crosses beneath them and to the right was the photo of the younger man and boys. She picked up a handful of dry-erase markers and under Doc's photo drew three lines: red, green, and yellow. She was certain the colours meant something.

Chester knocked on the door and entered excitedly. "I found him. Brandon Rakes, a.k.a. Richard Brandon." He hesitated, uncertain if he was intruding.

She waved him in. "What do we know?"

"Born 1952: Bristol, England. Emigrated to Canada with his mother in 1954, father killed in the Korean War. Attended university, majoring in kinesiology. He played centre-forward on the soccer team and was one of their top scorers. In the late '80s, he became a teacher and coached boys under-sixteen soccer. Taught at Lorne Minster College High School out west, and during his second year there they won the provincial championship. He left the school the following year, and then the trail goes cold."

She looked to the damaged photograph. "So, this is him?"

"I'd say yes."

She looked to the burnt edge. "How many kids comprise a team?"

"Eleven on the field," Chester said. "But any number could be feeding into an ad hoc team."

She moved the Polaroid under Rakes's morgue shot and drew a connecting line between the two images. She pointed to Doc's photo. "He's the next one for you to find. Arnold 'Doc' Wilson."

Harrison entered the room and Kes brought him up to speed. "We have a match on Rake: Richard Brandon. And a probable match that this is a photo of him as a young man. Chester's going to start tracking down Doc." She turned to Chester. "You have the address. I think we may find that Rake and Doc were close in age."

"And Doc was a stamp collector," Harrison added. "Rare stamps. Maybe that community knows him. He had to buy them somewhere."

Kes agreed. "It would have taken years to build that collection. A lifetime. Wherever he was buying them, he's been doing it for decades. Check the first volume of the collection. That's when he began."

Brownley entered, brushing away cookie crumbs from his jacket.

"We have a match on Brandon and the photo," Chester informed him. Brownley looked at the crosses on the board. "So they knew each other."

Kes didn't want them jumping to conclusions. "We don't know." She pointed to Doc's cross. "This one was intended to be found. Could be they're connected or they're a message for us. Maybe neither belonged to the victims, but were staged by the killers."

Brownley inspected the crosses. "No marks. No crucifixion symbol. Probably not Catholic, the line's too simple. An empty cross. Maybe Protestant or some associated denomination: Lutheran, Anglican, Presbyterian?" The group was staring at him. "What? I was a choirboy. We all were back then. Unlike you young heathens."

"What's that, a hundred years ago?" Chester chided him.

"Don't sass your elders." Brownley jabbed him in the arm.

"Watch it, old man. It'd be a shame for you to go out on disability."

Brownley mock-slapped at him, putting Chester on the defense, and in one swift move had him in a headlock under his arm. He rubbed his knuckles on his head like he was a kid.

Chester laughed. "Give! Give! Harrison, get him off me."

"Oh, you're with him?" Brownley waved him forward. "Come a little closer. Let me get a mitt on you."

"No friggin' way." Harrison backed off.

Kes watched them play. They needed the stress release. It was good to see them laughing. They were becoming a team. Her team.

Puck walked in and the men stood at attention. He hesitated, knowing he had interrupted something.

Kes smiled. "We were just wrapping up the day."

Puck didn't smile back. "Just letting you know the press is going to run with the story tonight. I can't keep them at bay any longer. Fear is going to rampage through this town. We're going to get overrun with false calls. Are we any closer?"

"No, sir," Kes said. "Not really."

"Do you think this is the last one?" He looked at her hopefully.

"No, sir."

He considered the board. "What's the Ethiopian flag have to do with it?"

"Sir?"

He pointed to the dry-erase marks. "Green represents the land, gold the sun, and red the blood that was spilled during colonialism."

Kes looked at the lines she'd drawn again. "I'm not sure. Those were the paint colours spilled on the stamp collections. Could be a coincidence."

Puck focused on his team. "Prepare yourself for media crossfire. Everybody will be looking for a story. I don't want any leaks from my precinct, understood?"

When he left, his gait was heavy and his shoulders bent.

"Do you still have the photos from this morning on your phone?" Chester asked.

Kes handed her cell over and he opened the app. She noted that he didn't need her passcode. "I remember seeing something—there!" He zoomed in on an image and focused on the background astern of Captain Phil's boat. "See...the buoys."

They were painted red, green, and yellow.

"Just because we're looking for patterns doesn't mean there is one," Kes said. She played the crime scene back in her head, unsettled that she hadn't noticed the buoys. "Good eye. Follow up."

XV.

KES WAS SITTING AT A TABLE FOR TWO, SIPPING A PINT AT THE DOG Hangs Low Pub and jotting down notes. The pages continued to fill with questions and a longer to-do list of follow-ups. She circled the word *cross* on the pages headed *Rake* and *Doc*.

She had just managed to get an order of scallop pasta before the kitchen closed. It seemed the chef was keen to get to a bingo game with a lucrative pot that was sure to go tonight. The pasta came with an impressive pile of pan-fried scallops on top. They were wonderful, so fresh and sweet. The city was only a two-hour drive away; why couldn't any of the restaurants there make anything as simple and perfect as this?

A young waitress, who still looked pert after the dinner rush hour, checked in: "Get you anything else?"

"Another pint, and please let the chef know this is delicious."

"Will do," she said, shooting a puzzled look at Kes. "Really?"

"Really."

The girl grimaced. "I hate scallops."

Some of the scallops were so large she had to cut them in half. She took a sip of water and felt that unease that someone was watching her. Her senses heightened, alert to her surroundings. When the waitress arrived with her beer, Kes took the opportunity to covertly check the bar. A man quickly turned his attention to the muted baseball game on TV. She studied his back. A flannel jacket, old workboots. Broad and stout. He was nursing a beer and she wondered if he was just curious or lonely.

She returned to her meal and her notes, both of which absorbed her attention. When she looked up again, the man was gone and his beer left unfinished.

"Excuse me." She waved the waitress over. "Do you know the man who was sitting at the bar?"

"No," she said. "But I've only been here a couple of weeks."

Kes decided to let it go. She knew she was being hyper-vigilant. It wasn't easy to shut it down, but Puck had ordered her to take the evening off. She was supposed to be setting stronger boundaries. Life is more than work, so she'd been told. She took her time finishing dinner, and then stepped into the chill of a spring night. There was a salty mist in the air that made the street lights blossom. In the muffled stillness, she could hear a distant truck and an intermittent foghorn far off at sea. The town felt peaceful and quiet, oblivious to the two corpses laying in the morgue and a missing woman, still unidentified.

She heard a scuff, stopped, and glanced behind her, but the street was empty. *A cat probably. Or a rat.* Even beautiful places had rats. She must be overtired.

She headed downhill, past her car, and strolled to the end of the pier. She could barely make out the lobster cars in the water. Farther out, she watched the lights of a boat recede. She looked to the misty glow of the houses edging the shore. It was uncomfortable to be so alone. As though everyone knew of an impending danger and was hiding. Or had simply disappeared, leaving only her behind.

Something splashed beneath her. Cautiously, she went to the wharf's edge and looked down. On a floating deck was an old man with a fishing pole and a flashlight pointed into the water. His rod bent and he reeled in his line. A soft glob flopped onto the deck and he scooped it into a bucket before unhooking the barb of his lure.

"What are you fishing?" she called down.

"Who wants to know?" He switched off his light.

"Just curious," she said.

The light came back on and shone up at her, blinding her, then swung back to the water.

"Squid," he answered.

"Do you fish here often?"

"Sure. Why not?"

"Did you happen to see a boat or lights at any of those lobster pens last night?"

"Be pretty crazy to visit another man's lobsters if you want to see daylight."

"So you don't get much theft?"

"People know what's theirs and what's not. You a cop?"

"Detective."

"Don't need a license for squid. Been coming here since I was a boy, so don't be trying to write me up."

"Wouldn't dream of it," she said. "Good luck."

"Don't need luck."

Kes headed back to her car. She wondered if the killers were brazen enough to have staged the crime in daylight. Take out a fishing boat and use its size to shield what they were doing. She stopped under a street light and made a note to find out how long the body had been in the water.

The killers had access to a boat. Knew about lobster pens, knew about the shooting competition, knew about the cabin, and the stamps...they knew a lot about this town. She breathed in the night and wondered why this place was the killing ground. What was it hiding?

She drove back to the motel thinking about a book she'd read as a kid. There had been an illustration of a giant squid with its tentacles wrapped around a schooner in a roiling sea. There were portholes in the boat and she remembered holding the book up close, trying to see the people inside. Did they know they were done for? Were they afraid? Were they holding onto each other?

That night, she dreamed she was swimming through murky waters. It was dark above and below, and she didn't know which way was shore. She floated on her back, trying to sense the way, when tentacles wrapped around her.

XVI.

KES WOKE GROANING. HER RIBS FELT LIKE THEY HAD BEEN CRUSHED IN a vise. She pushed herself upright and drew the courage to stand. A long, hot shower eased her muscles and she lingered under its soothing spray. She wiped the condensation from the mirror and gently dabbed away the blood crusted on the stitches. The bruising had softened. She combed her hair and pulled a fresh T-shirt and sweater from her suitcase. It took a long time to get them on. Her alarm sounded and she shut it off. She checked the clock on her phone, calculated the time difference, and placed the call.

It rang twice. Kes took a deep breath. "Hi. It's me." She shut her eyes and willed herself to be calm. "I know what time it is. I was hoping to talk to her, just for a moment." Her body stiffened. "No, I know that, I just hoped to catch her before..." Her eyes opened and she focused on the blue wall. "I can hear her." She bit her lower lip. "When then?" Tears welled. She mouthed *prick*, but her voice was sweet and calm. "Will you tell her I called, please? Tell her I'm thinking of her." But she knew he wouldn't. "Okay. Yeah, I heard you." She hung up and exhaled.

She rocked her neck side to side to release the stress. *It's your fault*, she told herself. *You did this.* A stronger voice in her head answered, *And you've paid.* She breathed it away and gently stretched. Pain cut across her ribs. She pushed harder, and forced her arm higher, until her body was screaming and she couldn't bear it anymore. *Stop*, the voice said. *Stop.*

Just before leaving for the station, she popped one of her pills and decided against the other. She pocketed it, just in case.

⋘⋯✦⋯⋙

Puck's car was already there, but she avoided his office and headed directly to the conference room. She wasn't ready for morning smiles and hellos. She perched on the table, opened her notebook, and flipped through her random notes. She jotted down a new list that spiralled into multiple, divergent columns, none of which connected. She had slipped deep into the rabbit hole of questions when her phone rang.

"Morris." Her team began to file into the room and she nodded to them as they entered. She listened for what seemed like a long time, staring at the floor.

"All right," she said. "Let me know...What do you want me to say? You fucked up. But you already know that."

She hung up and tossed her phone on the desk. She placed both hands on her knees and looked up.

"Morning, gentlemen. Half an hour ago, the groundskeeper was trimming shrubs around the hospital's back entrance by the staff parking lot and noticed what he thought was a clump of garbage. It was our missing Jane Doe. Her room was on the sixth floor directly above where she was found. Photos are being taken now. I'm not sure how useful they'll be for facial recognition."

"This isn't the MO," Brownley said. "This is reckless, panicked. Doesn't have the control of the others."

"Amateur." Kes agreed. "More like an underling or footguard cleaning up their mess."

"Maybe they're starting to decompensate," Harrison offered.

"Or escalate," Kes said.

Puck entered. "They call you?"

"Yeah."

"I told them to call you directly and take whatever shit came their way. Surveillance camera was down. No officer at the door. What the hell were they thinking? And how did they not find her sooner?" He noticed Kes's stillness. "You're surprisingly calm."

"We keep moving with what we have. Updates, gentlemen?"

The team shifted in their seats, also uncertain about her response to the news. Chester started: "I checked with Captain Phil on my way in this morning. The buoys were just buoys. He's had them forever."

"Good. Next?"

Brownley cleared his throat. "I met with George Swim last night. He runs the shooting club. I asked him about the judges. Two came from Millford Valley, but the third was an honorary judge for the day, a sort of thank-you position."

"Thank you for what?"

"He claimed to be a rep. He gave the club a new rifle, boxes of ammo, and a generous cash donation. Swim said he knew the company almost went out of business a couple of years back and was trying to reassert itself into the gun market, so he thought nothing of it. The guy seemed to be who he said he was."

"Chrissakes," Puck muttered and looked to Kes. "Whatever it takes, Detective. Oh, and you might want to leave the media to me. A simple 'no comment' will do, Crusher." He tossed the morning paper on the table and walked out.

She looked at the headline, MURDER IN THE HARBOUR, and a picture of her walking up the wharf with her quote beneath: "*I found out that lobsters...*" She chucked the paper into the garbage can.

"I don't want to hear it," she warned her team. "All right, we should get Jane Doe's photo shortly; Chester, work your magic."

Abruptly, Harrison stood. "I'm sorry. I have to go." He headed for the door.

"We're not done here." Her officers did *not* walk out on her.

For a moment, she thought he was going to keep walking, but then he turned. His face was flushed.

"I was there," he said. "With the killer. Feet away. I could have stopped this! Instead, I was focused on Mac and taking those rich bastards down a peg. I can't even describe what he looked like, and he handed my son the fucking bullets!"

Kes waited for him to finish venting. "So, you're pissed because you couldn't see what was coming?" She looked to Chester and Brownley. "If any of us could do that, we wouldn't be here, would we? There'd be no need for us to look back to figure out the how, who, and why. We'd be prophets, heroes, instead of picking up broken pieces and rooting through garbage. You're pissed because you're not a god, just a human."

She softened her tone. "All any of us have is *now*, Harrison. That's the job. That's what detectives do. We look backwards. We serve the dead. So, if you don't think you can do that job, you should leave."

Harrison returned to his seat.

Kes spoke to the team then as much as to herself: "The stress is going to keep mounting until we find whoever did this. I need you to take care of yourselves. I need you to stay focused and not get thrown by what-ifs. We can't spiral into what we can't change."

The room was silent. Brownley broke the mood. "I've been following up on Doc Wilson," he said, gently nudging them back to the case. "Officers went door to door last night. The closest neighbour said he kept to himself. Pleasant enough, but solitary. There's no indication he had a medical background. Once a year, a small group would come to his house. He'd inform the neighbours there'd be additional street parking that weekend. He said it was a philatelist society dropping in to trade and buy. I'm going to try to track them down."

Chester added, "The forensic team is going in today for Doc's prints and to check the paint cans in case the killers got sloppy."

"Good, good," Kes said. If they kept following the crumbs, they'd find the trail. "Brownley, can you go after the judges? See if they can come up with some kind of description, maybe have them sit with a sketch artist?"

"We don't have one in town, ma'am."

"Then do what you can. Take Chester with you. We know now that the killer can blend in. Based on the physicality of these murders and the level of intelligence and patience necessary to carry them out, I believe there's an alpha and a subordinate. The primary suspect is composed, maybe even affable, and likes to be close to see the results of his handiwork. Which also means he was likely nearby at the lobster pens watching us. Find out what boats were out there yesterday morning. Maybe our killers didn't stage the scene at night; maybe they just blended in with the other boats that day."

Harrison volunteered: "I'll get on the hunt for any reports of missing boats."

She was glad he was back in the game. Now, she needed to be honest with her team, if that's what she expected from them.

"This stays in the room. Last night, someone may have been watching me, maybe even following me. I only saw him from behind. Muscular, broad. Brown hair, medium build. I don't know how tall; he was seated. I'm not certain he was surveilling me, but I had the feeling."

She looked away, self-conscious that she had revealed that undefinable part of herself. But she also believed they each understood and trusted their own gut.

"We stick in pairs from now on. The killers know this town. They may be watching us. We know they like public displays and they don't like making mistakes. Jane Doe was a mistake."

The men nodded. Kes forced a smile; she didn't want fear to cloud their judgment. "Just be safe. Be aware."

Her phone beeped and she checked the message. "We have Jane Doe's face. Prints on all three victims are being run through the system. We'll be notified as soon as there's a match. Looks like the City's trying to kiss ass and make up."

XVII.

Kes waited at the end of the road leading to what remained of Rakes's cabin. Her damned ribs were throbbing, as though her body knew this was the place that had hurt her and was warning her away. She took another pill. She wanted her mind to be electric, to see what might have been missed.

The morning was warm and birds were careening through the trees, trying to lure her away from their nests. She breathed in the sweet smell of the woods. The green shoots of young ferns curled beneath shafts of light. The longer she looked, the more she noticed. Spiderwebs, sowbugs, exposed roots trailing over rock faces to disappear again under thin soil, stripped bark, woodpecker holes, how the branches didn't touch from tree to tree, how each species grew to the same height...

Harrison pulled in behind her.

She looked back to the cabin. The perimeter was cordoned off with caution tape.

"What are we after?" Harrison asked.

"Whatever we didn't see the first time. Let's start wide and come in." They split apart. Even though the grounds had been swept and cleared for explosives, Kes's stomach knotted and for the first few metres, she kept her eyes down looking for tripwire.

She had to force herself to keep stepping forward. Her body flushed hot and a cold sweat soaked her chest. Her heart was racing and she breathed through her mouth. *Calm down.*

"You okay?"

"Of course," she lied.

"The deer's been removed." Harrison was crouched where the remains had been. She flashed back to the deer tripping the wire and the wallop in her chest. He brushed away twigs. "There's quad tracks. Maybe someone took it for the pelt or dragged it off?" He followed the tracks to the edge of the woods. "They disappear here."

She stepped over the tangled trigger line that stretched across the property. They had used a fine copper wire, camouflaged by its surroundings. She found the tree trunk it had been tied to, just below knee height. She looked to the ground for footprints or cigarette butts, anything that could be a clue, but found nothing.

There were still wisps of smoke from hot spots on the site and a strong stench of burned plastic and wood. She stood at the threshold overlooking the ruins. Harrison joined her.

"Why blow this place up and loot the other house? Why go to all that trouble and risk?" she asked.

"To remove something that would lead us to them?"

"Or something that would connect the victims." She took inventory. "Both males lived alone. Isolated. Kept to themselves. About the same age. But lived within twenty miles of each other. Did they know each other? Had they met?"

"Maybe they were members of a club or the legion?"

"The photo we found suggests Rakes wasn't military." She looked around, taking in the scattered pots and damp, strewn clothes. "And there weren't any weapons in either house. No signs of additional security, locks, or cameras. Neither seemed to be living in fear."

She stepped into the rubble and walked the perimeter, scanning the foundation from every angle. The bed had been dragged off to the side. Harrison kicked through the debris where the books had been. He knelt down and looked closer. "I have something." Kes saw it: the corner of a photo that had slipped between the floorboards and the wall.

It was another black-and-white photo, of a young boy wearing swimming shorts standing next to a tire swing. There was a lake in the background and the boy was flexing his arm, show-ing off his muscles.

"A son?" Harrison suggested.

"Why do you say that?"

"The way it's shot. It's familiar. It's close. The boy is open. Playing. Happy. And the angle is higher, taken by someone taller." She looked to Harrison; it was a good observation. "They knew each other," he said.

"But why tucked into books? Not in frames? Or albums?" Kes asked.

"Maybe these were painful memories. Some kind of loss. Tragedy can break people. Make them want to retreat from the world."

Harrison's tone made Kes think he was talking about him-self. She looked out at the property and wondered what it would be like to live here. So solitary. This was where Rakes was taken from, she was sure of that.

This wasn't a man who had visitors. A knock on the door out here would be startling. He would have been on guard the moment he heard it, but the body showed no signs of physical struggle. Rakes didn't fight his killer. *Why not? How did they get you?* She walked to the middle of the room and looked to the trap door. What had been inside it?

Since they had last been there, the debris had been disturbed by officers, the bomb squad, the fire marshal. The kettle had been knocked over and the spout was facing the opposite direction. Shards of mugs had been kicked away to make a path. Animals had been here, too. Maple syrup, thick with flies, trailed over the floor and rug. Eggs had been dragged away, their shattered shells scattered about. Jars were open and cereal boxes ripped apart. *Raccoons? Bear?*

She walked to the trap door. Flies buzzed over it. Someone had neatly swept the debris away from around its frame.

"An animal didn't do that," Harrison said.

Kes bent down with difficulty. Noticing her wince, Harrison reached to steady her.

"I'm good," she said and lifted the door.

Inside, black milky eyes stared back. The neck stained with blood and maggots. The doe's severed head.

Harrison took a step back. "What the hell?"

Kes stood and slowly turned, staring hard into the woods and dappled light, trying to sense if they were being watched. She peered into the shadows and inhaled deeply, trying to catch the scent.

XVIII.

ON THE DRIVE BACK TO REVISIT DOC'S HOUSE, KES'S ATTENTION WAS ON the ocean inlets slipping past. The sparkle of water, hard shale borders, and patches of seagrass evoked someplace wild and untamed. Amidst the bouldered shores were small white sand beaches. Her car hugged the winding curves. The beauty of the place washed away the ugliness of the world. Or maybe it just distracted and hid it better. But no, she had seen the crime statistics. This was a place that rarely saw inconceivable violence. It was a place people came to feel safe.

Harrison was following close behind. She took a left at the four-way and passed the gas station, convenience store, and laundromat, and entered the town proper. She remembered the turn up the hill, even before Harrison put on his turn signal to forewarn her. A police car was in the driveway. Doug and Sally, patrol officers who doubled as the local detachment's forensics team, were there. Kes doubted their credentials. They only had a handful of courses and city conferences, but Puck had assured her they were keen and thorough.

Kes donned gloves and booties and let herself in. She didn't wait for Harrison. He knew what to do. He had downstairs today and she was taking up. Fresh eyes.

The hidden doorway was open and Doug and Sally were inside, dusting the paint cans for prints. They were so intent on their work they didn't notice her at the door. They moved with minute precision.

"Any luck?"

"It looks like they were wiped down." She could only see Sally's eyes over her mask. Young eyes.

Harrison joined her. The team nodded his way.

"We have two hardware stores in town that sell paint," Harrison said. "I can try to match the brands, maybe even the paint lots, if you can grab me a sample."

"Will do," Sally said.

Doug handed Kes an envelope. "We found this under the table. Maybe it fell out before the others were destroyed." Inside were two stamps in protective sheets. "It seems like the collection was all marine-related. Ships, schooners, sailboats."

She passed the envelope to Harrison.

"You should be careful with that," Doug said. "It could be valuable. My father was an amateur collector. He liked birds. Bought his stamps at the post office every year. Nothing too expensive." He looked to the albums caked in dried paint. "But this was serious collecting."

"Would it have been worth anything?" Kes asked.

"Could be hundreds of thousands here. Some of these are really old and, I suspect, rare."

"Really? For stamps?" Harrison said.

"It's a passion. An obsession. For some, it's a love. People will pay anything for their obsessions." He kept his gloved hands up like a surgeon. "There are stories about collectors buying the last known stamps in the world and destroying all but one."

"The killer knew the victim's heart's desire," Kes said, and headed upstairs. "Keep an eye out for cubbyholes and nooks. Check under rugs."

As she climbed the stairs, the sound muted. The dark oak panels and bags of cat litter stored on the treads made the crammed space seem smaller. Her chest tightened. She breathed out and focused on the light at the top of the landing. She breathed deeper when she reached the top and the hallway widened. At the end of the hall a small, fly-specked window dimly glowed. The house felt empty, joyless, and she suspected it always had. The wide floorboards creaked underfoot. If Doc had been grabbed from up here, he would have heard someone coming up the stairs. The cat might even have alerted him. It was skittish enough.

The stench of cat litter grew as Kes approached the bathroom. The litter box was full. Three days since it had been emptied? Maybe more? *How long were victims kept before they were killed?* A small claw foot tub was draped by a plastic curtain hanging from the ceiling. It was too small for a tall man. The enamel was chipped and scummy and there were small splotches of mould on the curtain. One corner of the medicine cabinet mirror was cracked and the door hung slightly off its hinge. It creaked when she opened it. Inside were various medications, unopened boxes of toothpaste, and over-the-counter acetaminophen. There were multiple names on the prescription labels. *What are these for, Doc?*

She hollered downstairs: "Harrison, there are pill bottles in the bathroom. Can you bag them when you're done?"

"Copy that," he called back.

The outer walls of the bedroom were stacked high with magazines. The bedding was a twist of greyed sheets and a grimy comforter. *You didn't sleep easy.* She lifted up the mattress, flipped over the pillows, and checked under the bed. Nothing but cat hair and lost coins.

In the closet were work shirts, sweaters, and pants of meagre and poor quality. A few shirts still had thrift store tags. *Why did you live like this when you had so much?* There was nothing in the closet corners or the shelf above where boxes could have been tucked away. She tapped along the inside walls listening for the hollow thud that might indicate a hidden space, but it sounded solid. Her phone rang.

"Morris." She ran her fingertips down the line of clothing shoulders, not yet ready to leave the victim.

"Kes. Captain Puck. We have an ID on Jane Doe's photo. Susan recognized her. She's known as Miss Olson, lived in the

Little Bend Campground about eight or nine kilometres north of town. We had to pay her a visit a few years ago. Set fire to a tire outside one of her neighbours' trailers trying to smoke out an old guy she said was peeping on her. Claimed it was an accident."

"Okay, we'll head there next," she said and hung up.

She took a moment in the dark, sad room of the victim. She asked the emptiness, "Did you know your killers?" But the house wasn't giving up its secrets.

She stepped into the hall and stood at the top of the stairs. The thumbnail where the cross had been hung was directly overhead. She reached up, but had to stand on tiptoe.

She felt a coldness under her hand. She was standing where the killer had stood. "You're tall," she said quietly. "And you've been here before, haven't you? How long were you watching him?"

She heard only the buzz of flies trapped against windows. The longer she listened, the more acute her hearing became. She could discern each fly and the rhythm of its wings. She could tell which were exhausted and which were still fighting.

Her breathing had deepened. She pressed her thumb against the tack hole. She looked down to where the chain would have hung and the silver cross at her eyeline, and felt only an icy deadening inside.

XIX.

THEY PASSED OVER THE BRIDGE SPANNING THE MAIN HIGHWAY AND THE road narrowed. They were travelling inland through dense forest that fanned into rolling farmland then shuttered back to impenetrable bush. It made Kes think of the settlers who had hacked through this woodland to create pastures for their animals. She couldn't comprehend how that was possible with just hand tools and a few oxen.

She wasn't accustomed to being a passenger and tried not to fidget as Harrison took a hard right at the bottom of the hill. The truck had a heaviness and bounce to it, suggesting the springs were sagging from too many off-road stints.

The coffee holder was ringed with spills and the steering wheel was glossy where it had been gripped for years. The interior was shabby—not dirty, just well-worn; this was a utilitarian vehicle, a working truck that would never let you down. *Much like its owner*, she thought. Tucked in the visor was a photo of Harrison and his son taken several years back. Mac was hoisting a fish up to the camera.

They transitioned onto a well-maintained dirt road that snaked through a pine forest. The acidity of the fallen needles had burned away any other vegetation. Kes rolled down her window and breathed in deeply.

Harrison slowed when the road passed over a stream and the forest gave way to a well-mowed field where several recreational trailers were parked in designated spots, ringing a lake. There was small beach, perhaps man-made, with an old waterslide.

At the lakeshore, two men were putting out docks for the summer. Beside them, an old tractor idled. The scene reminded Kes of when she had first become a detective and had access to all the police resources. She spent her first vacation tracking down her mother, who had left when she was twelve. She found her in a campground not unlike this one, where she was living with her partner. Kes hadn't confronted her. Hadn't even shown herself. She had just watched them. Two women who had found love.

Her mother's friend had an awkward way of moving, as though her knee or foot pained her, but that didn't seem to hinder her energy and enthusiasm. They were barbecuing outside their trailer. Her mother smiled and laughed often. She seemed happy. She didn't appear to miss her daughter at all. Kes watched them until the light got low and the women retreated from the mosquitoes into the camper. When Kes finally drove away, she had to pull over because she couldn't see through her tears. That was the last time Kes cried for her mother, or herself.

Harrison pointed. "That's the owner down there at the beach. I'll see if he has a key to Olson's place."

Kes got out and stretched. Most of the larger trailers, with porches and overhangs built on, were situated close to the forest's edge facing the lake. They were spaced farther apart than the smaller lots, which she gathered were for summer visitors. At the park entrance were three low log cabins: a canteen, gift shop, and office. Up the hill, tucked deeper into the woods, she could make out another trailer. *Apart. Alone.* She guessed it would be Missy Olson's.

Harrison returned. "It's lot one hundred."

"The one up there."

"Yeah. How did you...?" But she was already walking toward it.

From the crest of the hill, Kes could take in much of the park, but the wend of the path and seclusion of the trees camouflaged the trailer. As she approached, she saw a home in disrepair. Beneath the windows were small wooden plant boxes that appeared to have been empty for years. A crooked wooden porch led to an aluminum door that needed replacing. The pale green siding was rusting in spots and garbage bags of leaves surrounded it.

Harrison followed her gaze. "Insulation," he said.

"What don't you see?"

"No vehicle," he said.

"No vehicle," Kes repeated.

A well-worn footpath skirted the trailer into the back woods. Two squirrels raced out from a stack of firewood and bolted up a tree.

The campsite owner arrived on a ride-on lawn mower, which seemed small for his size. "I've got the key," he said, hobbling toward them. He was out of breath from the short, soft incline. Kes glanced to his feet. His ankles were swollen and she wondered about his heart.

"Where the hell's Miss Olson?" He reminded her of a bull.

"I'm sorry to tell you, she was found dead this morning."

"Murdered?"

Kes stepped toward him. "Why would you assume that?"

"She was a nasty lady, seen her make folks cry. Sometimes people get what they deserve."

"What's your name?"

"I ain't done nothin'."

"I'd just like to know who I'm chatting with."

"Parker."

"Mr. Parker?"

"Nah. Parker up front. Parker McNeil."

"And Miss Olson's first name?"

"Miss, I thought. Short for Missy? She was from one a them Europe countries. Norwege or something."

"Melissa, maybe," Kes said to Harrison. "Did she have a car, Parker?" She gave him her full attention like he was very important, his every word germane. Harrison stood off to the side and watched her work him.

"'Course she did. It's a bitch getting a taxi 'round these parts."

"What did she drive?"

"A little beater—2004 Nissan. Painted the same green as the trailer. Loved that colour, she did. Asked me to paint it for her when she first moved in, the trailer that is, back in the nineties. She was nice then. And nice to look at. But it was all show to get what she wanted. She turned quick after that. Like a badger."

Parker tucked in his shirt and pulled up his pants. He retrieved a huge ring of keys from his plaid jacket pocket and walked up the steps to the metal door. He had to jiggle the key and pull up on the door to release the lock. He pushed it open. "Christ almighty. Someone's been rooting through here."

"If you could wait outside, please," Kes said.

"This is my property. Anything left behind, including contents, belongs to me."

"I'm sure you don't want to hinder or interfere with an investigation, Parker. You've been so helpful thus far." Kes waited for his gaze to move from her chest to her eyes. "You can help us by ensuring that nobody, including you, enters this trailer. Otherwise, that would be a criminal offence."

"I'm here to help, yes I am."

"If you could wait down by your mower, Parker. We don't want the area trampled. Could be clues."

Parker looked down to his feet. "Yeah, of course." He lifted his feet high and carefully stepped away. Harrison looked to her, surprised she hadn't just ordered him to back off.

Kes found the light switch, and a row of overhead moon lamps with halogen bulbs popped on, flickered, then held. She drew back the main curtain to let in more light. The floor was strewn with clothes and paperbacks and all the cupboards had been opened. Empty bottles of wine and vodka were piled around the dining table where an old television had pride of place. She walked over the mounds of junk to the back bedroom. It was in the same state of disarray. She pulled back the heavy curtains above the bed to reveal a lovely view of the lake. Dust drifted through the band of light.

She returned to the front door and called out to Parker: "Did Miss Olson ever have guests over?"

"No way. It was like she had Bugger Off written on her fore-head. No animals neither. No flowers. Nothing alive, really. She was a sad and bitter woman who liked the bottle."

"Did she ever go out?"

"Sometimes. Rare though. She'd put on a dress. Only reason a feller like me noticed. She normally wore all kinds of baggy crap, but she had a good set of legs. Real good."

Kes stepped back into the trailer. Harrison was leafing through an old book.

"What is it?"

"Lesson plans. Published 1973. A teacher's handbook. Maybe she taught where the picture of the boys was taken?"

She turned to the door. "Parker." He stood up straighter and sucked in his belly. She noticed he had smoothed back his hair. "Was Miss Olson a teacher?"

"God help 'em kids if she was. I had ones like her. Would tear a strip off you as soon as look at you. Mean. Just plain mean."

"Kes." Harrison, standing before a mirror strung with cheap necklaces, pulled off the first chain and held it up.

A small silver cross.

XX.

ON THE WHITEBOARD, KES WROTE *"MISS" OLSON* BENEATH HER PHOTO. She stepped back and looked at the three contorted faces of Miss, Doc, and Rakes. A map had been added, marking the crime scenes and victims' houses. She circled the campground. The only visible pattern was that all three victims were located in the same county and had lived in isolation. Harrison pinned up the photo of the young boy beside the Polaroid of the soccer team and added the third cross to the board.

Puck joined them, followed by Chester and Brownley. Everyone seemed weary. They were doing the legwork and getting nowhere, which wore on morale.

"All right," said Kes. "Who wants to start?"

Brownley volunteered. "Chester and I are just back from meeting with the two judges from the shooting range. Neither had seen the guest judge before, but said he knew his guns and spoke like a sales rep. Their descriptions were thin. He wore glasses, which they both said might have been more for fashion; they weren't sure he needed them. He had a way of looking over the frames when he was talking and took them off when he got in his car. He also had on a ballcap, no logo. They couldn't agree on his eye colour. He was over six feet, but not much over, and had light brown or dirty blond hair. Lean, but well built. Thirty to forty. They weren't good at estimating age. Middle, they said."

Kes jotted down notes. "Did they notice what kind of car he drove? Was it a pale green?"

"Yes." Brownley looked at her curiously. "He told them a friend had loaned it to him for the weekend and that he was flying back west the following day. They thought it was an odd choice for a big honcho gun representative."

She looked to Puck. "Let's put out an APB on Olson's car."

"It's a 2004 Nissan," said Harrison.

"I'll get the plate number," Chester added.

Brownley continued. "I checked on missing boats, but nothing has been reported yet. We've expanded the search up and down the shore and the Coast Guard has been notified, in case a vessel was abandoned at sea or sunk."

"After Harrison called, we also checked on the paint. It wasn't bought locally. Or nobody remembers taking the order."

Brownley flipped through his notes. "And nothing is back on prints or DNA. It's possible none of the victims are in the system. That's about it...Nothing."

"Harrison?" To his surprise, Kes passed their report over to him.

He didn't hesitate. "We revisited Rakes's cabin. There were quad tracks and the deer's remains were gone. We later found its severed head in the previously empty, or emptied, hidden cubby."

Kes looked to Puck. "The killers returned and are staying close, indicating they aren't done yet." Not what he wanted to hear.

Harrison pointed to the board. "We also found another photograph."

The men got up to take a closer look at it.

"Do you think it could be one of the boys from the soccer team, Chester?" Kes asked.

"Maybe, a couple of years older. I'll run an analysis."

Harrison carried on, "We then went to Doc's house for an additional search. Nothing further was discovered. Though we do have a stash of prescription pills with different names on them. And..." He reached in his pocket. "Two undamaged stamps were found." He handed the evidence bag to Kes, who placed it under Doc's photo.

"We also located 'Miss,' possibly Melissa, Olson's trailer. A third cross was found there. As we know, her car is missing. She was a loner, but left a couple times a year for short stints." Harrison closed his notes and looked to Kes.

"And we found a teacher's manual," Kes prompted.

"Yes, from the seventies." Harrison wasn't pleased he had missed something.

Kes mapped out the next steps. "Let's start checking out motels within a fifty-kilometre radius. See if anyone fitting the gun rep's description has rented a room in the last weeks. And get me a list of all the schools in the area. Let's try to figure out where Olson came from. We know we're dealing with more than one killer. They're covering too much ground for this to be a solo job." She pondered the logistics of the crime scenes. "It even seems too much for two people..."

"Do you think there's a religious connection? Should we be checking out churches?" Brownley asked.

"There's nothing in the staging of the crimes that suggests religious rituals. The crosses were brought to the scenes. They mean something to the killers. Maybe they see themselves as doing God's work and this is their calling card? Or maybe they're just trying to muddy the trail. My gut says follow the boys. I want to know who they are. Focus on the schools first."

Brownley said wearily, "It doesn't feel like we're getting any closer."

"We are, though." Kes rallied the energy to convince them and herself. "We just don't know what we're getting closer to yet. They're either toying with us or setting down directional markers leading us *to* or *away* from something. We keep following. Any questions?" The men remained quiet. "Rest up tonight. We'll go hard at it again tomorrow."

They shuffled out with the dissatisfaction of a day that had led nowhere. Kes stayed behind. As did Puck.

"You should head home, too," he said.

She continued writing down an action plan. "We haven't found cellphones or computers at any of the crime scenes. We need to contact phone companies and reverse-track their numbers, try to match them up by names, addresses, and get into the logs—check incoming and outgoing calls. Maybe Chester can use a locator? And same with emails, servers; we can pull in the Cyber Unit for help." Her mind was unspooling all the possible threads.

"It'll wait until tomorrow," Puck said.

"But if we get on it tonight—"

She glanced up at the board, searching for anything they'd overlooked. It was so easy to miss the bigger picture when you were focused on the microscopic.

"Kes." He stopped her. "That's the day."

She looked to the victims' photos. "Not for the killers."

XXI.

Kes choose a stool at the pub's bar. She didn't bother with the menu; she knew what she wanted. There was a long mirror on the wall across from her, so she could observe what was going on behind her. The Dog Hangs Low was much busier than the other night and the sound of laughter relaxed her somewhat. She ordered a pint, and while she waited noticed a newspaper tucked to the side. She flipped it over to read the front page.

High-profile city detective brought in for local crime. Morris told this reporter that all she's found out so far is that "lobsters have two claws, a pincer and crusher, and it's the crusher you need to worry about." Well, "Crusher," get on it...

Kes rolled her eyes. No wonder Puck was pissy this morning. Reporters could be such assholes.

The waitress returned with a loaded tray and set Kes's beer on the counter. "It's a decent photo," she commented. "I'll be right back for your order."

Kes slid the paper away. That explained the looks she was getting walking in. Everyone knew everyone's business in this town, but three murders and she didn't have a single lead.

The bar was getting rowdier and the voices louder. She searched in the mirror for the source. One of the scallop draggers had come home and a few of the crew were swapping tales with some younger men from a sailing schooner. Their table was laden with pitchers of draft. One of the men was already staggering. The waitress sidestepped him to lay down a tray of beer. He was in a heated explanation, broadly miming his points for emphasis. The recipient of his story looked unimpressed.

Kes took a long drink of her cold beer. It was exactly what she needed. She wished she could sit here all night and nail them back until she stopped thinking. But she had taught herself restraint long ago, after a bad stretch of one-night stands and blackout binges. Drinking made her aggressive and angry, punishing and self-destructive. An exorcism of all the shit she'd seen. Once she woke up in an alley, not knowing how she'd gotten there, and ended it. Running was her vice now. If she was going to punish herself, at least she'd be in good shape. These days, her limit was two beers.

"Sorry," the waitress said. "What can I get you?"

"Fish tacos and another beer when you come back. And some hot sauce, please."

"Coming up." She pushed her way through the crowd back to the kitchen.

Odd how the world went about its business despite the gruesome murders happening just outside the door. Kes savoured her beer and looked at her reflection in the mirror. Her eye was looking better. The bruise was fading, but the stitches were starting to itch.

Over her shoulder, Kes noticed a man who seemed to be staring at her. She looked away and focused on her beer, trying to recall the back of the man from the other night. Similar build, brown hair. It was the slope of his shoulders that seemed familiar...She glanced up. He was looking directly at her.

She pretended to answer her phone and discreetly switched it to camera mode while lifting it to her ear. She faked a conversation while shooting photos of the man in the mirror, careful not to let her eyes give anything away.

Someone slammed against her, almost knocking her beer over. An elbow grazed her tender ribs and she jumped up from her stool.

The drunken storyteller swiped at his shirt; he'd spilled his beer when he bumped into her. "What the fuck?" he said, like it was her fault. Kes grabbed his shirt at the collar and twisted the material hard, choking it to his neck. She pulled him low and close and shoved her badge in his face.

"I've had a shit day. If you don't piss right off, I'll have you tossed out, or do it myself. Now get back over there and sit down!"

She let go of his shirt and pushed him away with her fingertips. He staggered back. The room had grown quiet and people were waiting for what would happen next. Kes stared the drunk down and rooted her feet, preparing for an attack. Her muscles tingled and her fists clenched.

Her eyes said *Try me, and I will hurt you.* One of his buddies grabbed him by the shoulder and hauled him back to the table. She ignored the mumbled *bitch* and sat back down. A few patrons clapped.

Kes's body was buzzing and her hands shook a little. She breathed softly to calm herself. She had wanted the drunk to resist. She had wanted an excuse to pummel him. She looked to the mirror for her suspect and wasn't surprised he was gone.

"Here you go." The waitress set her dinner down. "All we have is Tabasco. Hope that's okay. Owner says it's on the house, Crusher."

Kes pulled into the Jib's parking lot, aching for the hot steam of the shower and the soft sheets of the bed. Her evening at the pub hadn't been the relaxing one she'd hoped for, but her muscles were a bit less tense from the three pints. One over her limit, but she'd earned it.

She abruptly braked. The lights were on in her motel room. She shut off her car and was instantly sober. She got out and cautiously approached, stepping in close to the wall. The door was closed and the lock intact. No sign of it being jimmied. She could hear what sounded like furniture scraping the floor, but couldn't see through the drawn curtains. She pulled out her phone and called Harrison.

"Hello?"

"Kes here," she whispered. "There's someone in my room. I can't see in."

"Wait for me. Don't move."

She fought the urge to charge in. *Be the grouse,* her father would say. *Take cover and wait. Don't be the pheasant that bolts full-tilt into a line of buckshot.*

She quieted her mind and listened. The sounds coming from inside sharpened. She could hear where the intruder was in the room.

She scanned the parking lot looking for vehicles that she hadn't clocked earlier, but the same pickups and work trucks were in their designated spots. *Be the grouse.* She counted the seconds in her mind into minutes, until Harrison's truck sped into the lot at three minutes and forty-three seconds.

He jumped out wearing pyjama bottoms, a T-shirt, and his chest holster. She indicated for him to take the other side of the door and that there was one person inside. She pointed to the back right corner.

He pulled his weapon and Kes signalled in three, two, one. He kicked the door open.

"Police. Freeze!"

Crouched in the corner, an old woman raised her hands in surrender: "Don't shoot! Don't shoot!"

"Lower your weapon, Harrison," said Kes. "She's the owner."

They had just barged in with a weapon drawn on a seventy-year-old woman in a purple track suit with curlers in her hair. Harrison's adrenaline was pumping as he lowered his gun.

"Hazel, you can get up." Kes helped the trembling woman to her feet. "You can put your arms down. What are you doing in here?"

The bedsheets were on the floor, the mattress half off the box spring, the contents of Kes's suitcase strewn about.

"I'm so sorry. I was taking Constance for her walk and noticed your lights on and the door ajar. I came to see if you were all right and I found it like this...I was trying to set it right. I didn't want you to come back to this."

"You should have called the police."

"Yes, I should have." She looked pale and unsteady. "But I saw the mess and thought, oh dear, your things and..."

"It's okay. We'll take it from here, Hazel. You should go make yourself a tea and stay with Constance. We'll straighten it up."

"I can walk you back to your room," Harrison offered.

Kes noticed how easily he had switched to a gentle calm.

"No, you stay, dear. This has never happened before. Breaking into a room. Do you think they could come back?"

Kes led Hazel to the door. "No, I think they're gone."

Hazel looked to the parking lot. "It's an awful feeling. I don't even lock my doors."

"Try not to worry about this. I'll check on you in the morning," Kes promised and shut the door softly behind her.

Harrison slid the mattress onto the bed. He looked around the room to see what else he could straighten and saw Kes's underwear lying beside her suitcase; he averted his eyes.

She tossed the sheets onto the mattress, followed by the pillows, then kicked the box spring back into place. She kicked it again and again. "Fuck." She clutched her ribs.

"We should find you another motel. Leave your car at the station."

"No." Kes picked up her underwear and shirts and stuffed them back into the suitcase. "They're showing themselves. They know who I am. Why I'm here. They're trying to scare me away? Warn me to back off? No. Now we know how close they are, and that they still have something to finish."

"You shouldn't stay here, Kes. Puck is going to—"

"We're not going to tell Puck about this."

"Kes..."

"That's an order." She heard the aggression in her voice. "I'm sorry," she said. "Please go home. I'm fine."

"We're supposed to be a team," he said.

"I thought that's why I called you."

Harrison stared hard at her, trying to read what was hidden in her eyes, but she had locked herself away. He slammed the door on his way out.

XXII.

Kes woke tangled in the comforter. Soft morning light edged the curtains. It had taken her hours to fall asleep, and when she finally did, she kept waking, thinking there was someone in the room. She lowered herself onto the floor and half-heartedly stretched, but her ribs were aching. She hated that she couldn't run. It's what helped keep her sane.

The shower was lukewarm and her clothes were wrinkled, having been crammed back into the suitcase. She looked like she felt. She'd have to find time to talk to Harrison. He was right; they were supposed to be a team, and she was still acting solo. It was a balance she could never quite strike.

Teammate, leader, woman, detective. This is how they saw her. But she thought of herself more like an animal hunting its prey. When she finally got inside the skin—could see through their eyes and feel their pulse in hers—there wasn't room for anyone but the killer and her. Not even those she loved. She pushed away the word she had omitted. *Mother.* That word was separate. She didn't keep it with the others.

She was supposed to be mentoring Harrison. He was a good cop, she knew this now. *She* was the one straddling the line. If she was being honest, she drew her own line to suit herself.

She had missed a stray sock on the floor from last night, picked it up and stuffed it back in the suitcase beside her crumpled underwear. The killer had left them on the floor on purpose so she'd know he'd seen them, touched them. For the first time, she felt the violation of all those who had experienced the same.

She had stood on the other side as a police officer nodding in empathy, but she had never truly understood the victim's pain and fear. That was how she protected herself. Now someone was trying to intimidate her. *Fuck that.*

She shoved the underwear deeper into her suitcase, reached in her jacket, and retrieved her pills. She took two.

She quieted the growl in her body and practised a smile. She had promised to check on Hazel. Then she would hunt.

Her unit was already waiting for her in the conference room. Kes looked to Harrison, but he didn't meet her eyes. Susan was setting out a basket of muffins on the table alongside fruit and coffee. Kes was hungry and the muffins looked homemade.

"I wasn't sure if everyone was eating properly," Susan said. "The coffee's from home. It's all freshly made."

It smelled wonderful. "Thank you, Susan." Kes caught her glance to Brownley on her way out and his wink back.

Kes took up position at the front of the room. "Good morning, everyone. Shall we begin?"

Puck spoke first. "We may have a break. Last night, a squad car coming in from highway patrol spotted Olson's car. The officer had to take a leak and there it was on a lay-by off the main road. Doug and Sally are on scene."

"Can we get it towed here, Captain? Keep it out of sight?"

"Not a problem."

"Harrison, you stay with forensics. Have them strip the car completely. Maybe they left something behind. Chester, what's happening with prints? DNA?"

"Nothing back from the lab, and prints aren't getting any hits in the database. Identities still unknown. That photo you brought in yesterday of the boy, I'll be running aging programs to compare with the group photo today."

Kes fired up her phone. "I have another one I want you to print..."

Chester's phone dinged and he opened the file. "It's pretty dark. Is that the pub? And is that you?"

Puck interjected, "What's this about, Kes?"

"Person of interest." She looked to Harrison, who held her gaze. He wasn't going to say anything. "Just being cautious, sir. I'll inform you if there's anything to be concerned about."

"I also have a lead that might help us," Brownley offered. "I checked with local motels like you asked. There's one, The Brigantine. Owner says one of their guests has been there for a week. He's taken a room there before, for the same length of time. Tall man, around forty, sandy hair. They don't know anything about him, he keeps a low profile. Doesn't seem to be a tourist. He's booked through till tomorrow."

"Okay." *Finally a break.* She looked to Brownley. "You and I will take a couple officers over there and pay him a visit." The sweet buzz of the pills was kicking in. That, and the thrill of a scent to follow. "Tell the officers not to approach until we get there. No sirens. And call the owners, let them know we're coming—and not a word."

"Copy that," Brownley said.

"Okay, boys, let's fuel up," she said. "Grab a coffee and muffin."

She could feel the rush of energy in the room as the men swarmed the treats and filled their mugs. For the first time, they weren't trailing behind. Something was about to happen.

XXIII.

"He's in room fourteen," Brownley said. "How do you want to play this?"

"Send the officers around back in case he tries to leave. We'll take the front, knock, and see if he'll let us in. That's all we can do without exigent circumstances." Sometimes the law was a pain in the ass. "He might not even be our guy, but keep sharp." Kes put on her bulletproof vest. "If it is him, he's dangerous."

The motel was long and low, like an old Midwestern highway stop. It stretched back on the property farther than Kes had expected. Wooden chairs were placed outside each door beneath a slightly sloped roof that overhung the walkway. A neon sign pointed to the office.

Brownley sent the police officers to take their positions and joined Kes to flank the door. A television was on loud, arguing voices and sinister music. She knocked.

Brownley had his weapon at ready. She knocked again louder. On the TV music heightened and a woman screamed, like she was being murdered.

"Sounds like exigent circumstances to me." Kes looked to Brownley.

"Sounds like someone's in trouble," Brownley agreed. "I heard a scream."

Kes stepped back and Brownley kicked open the door just as a man opened it.

"Police! Hands up, hands up!"

"What the hell?" The man was holding his nose, blood seeping between his fingers. "You can't just—"

"Baby? Oh my god, what's happening?" A woman wrapped in a white towel stepped out from the bathroom. A cloud of steam followed her.

"Hands up!" Brownley ordered the woman and then lowered his weapon. "Mayor Wallace?"

"This is illegal," she shrieked. "I'll have your nuts! Get the hell out of here!"

Brownley looked to Kes for direction.

"Sorry, ma'am. We heard screams of a woman in distress," she said. "We're working a murder case, as you may have heard, and looking for a suspect. This gentleman fits his description. You understand the urgency and special privileges we have in this case. I believe the order was signed by you." She focused on the man. "What's your name?"

"You can't barge into our room!" The woman's towel had slipped, exposing a blush of nipple. Kes touched her own chest and the mayor yanked up her towel.

Kes turned down the TV. "If you want to call your lawyer, we can wait for him to arrive. Of course, the media might get wind of it."

"I'm Mark Driscoll," the man said.

"And why are you visiting town, Mr. Driscoll?"

He looked to the mayor. His face reddened. He wasn't their man. Their man wouldn't show shame.

"Mind if Detective Brownley here takes a look at your driver's licence?"

"In my jacket pocket. Hanging on the rack over there."

Brownley went to the coat, reached in the side pocket, and pulled out a wallet. He leafed through until he found the man's license. He nodded affirmative to Kes.

"Please excuse our intrusion. Have a nice day."

The door slammed behind them. There was going to be hell to pay.

"Probably wise to keep that one to yourself," Kes advised.

"Christ, that'll be hard," Brownley said. "Her husband's on my curling team."

Kes took off her vest and tossed it in the backseat of Brownley's car. "Send the officers home."

"Sorry, boss. I should have dug deeper," he said.

"This isn't on you, Brownley. I'm the one who gave the order to go in. Understood?"

"You don't have to do that," Brownley protested.

"It's what happened." That was the end of it.

Kes had Brownley drop her off at the impound gate, and headed towards the outbuilding where the car was being searched. Her phone rang.

"Detective, it's Connie Hawthorne. I've been talking to the City Medical Examiner and there's preliminary information on the Olson file I thought you would want sooner than later."

"Go ahead."

"She had the same drug in her system as the other shooting victim. Two bullets made impact. There was brain damage and it was unlikely she would have regained consciousness. She was non-responsive on the Glasgow Scale. But it was the impact from the fall that broke her neck."

The killers took a big risk to silence someone who would never talk. Kes could hear Connie flipping through her notes.

"She was probably around sixty years old. Same needle entry in her upper thigh as the others. No physical bruising or sign of struggle."

"Sexual assault?"

"No indication of it."

"Distinguishing marks?"

"A tattoo on her left wrist. A playing card. I've sent you a photo." Kes checked her phone. The ace of clubs. "By the fade of the ink and stretching of skin, I'd say it's quite old." Connie paused. "She was also pierced."

"Where?"

"Both nipples and the labia..."

Kes heard a hesitation. "And...?"

"There's another tattoo, scrolled across her pelvis. It says *Punish me*. Your victim was into pain. I'll send photos."

"Thanks, Connie." Kes forwarded the playing card image to Chester with the message, MEANING? ON OLSON.

Piece by piece, she thought. "One more question, Connie. Do you have a sense of how long Doc Wilson was in the lobster car?"

"Just a sec. I was just finishing those calculations..." Kes held. The sun was warm and she lifted her face to its heat. Her shoulders relaxed.

Connie came back on the line, "Minimal bloating, no skin sloughing, the water temperature is still cold...no more than six hours, I'd think."

Earlier than Kes had thought. Around midnight or shortly after. Around the same time their Jane Doe was tossed out a window? "Can you get me an approximate time of death for Olson?"

"Will do," Connie said. "You think there's multiple killers?"

"Not ruling out any possibilities. Appreciate it, Connie."

Kes hung up and headed over to the impound building. Sally was crouched by the driver's side of the car and Doug was under the chassis. The doors and interior panels had been removed and the tires were off. Harrison was leaning into the trunk, searching through the spare-wheel well.

"How's it going?" she asked.

Harrison straightened, knocking his head on the trunk. He stepped back and pulled off his mask and gloves. He was drenched in sweat.

"We found a handgun taped up here, over the spare tire. Serial number filed off. I handed it over to Puck."

"Good." She smiled at Sally, who was cutting away the carpet. Doug wheeled out from under the chassis. He pulled down his mask. He looked like a Ph.D. student.

"We have a lot of fingerprints," Doug said. "Most likely belonging to the victim, based on the patterns of use—steering wheel, radio, cupholder, handle. There are others on the passenger side, maybe just friends'. There is a second set on the driver's side...but they won't be of much use to us."

"Why not?"

"There are no actual prints. Just marks. The finger pads are obscured."

"They've been altered?"

"Possibly. Abraded, burned, cut..." There was concern in the young officer's eyes.

Kes hadn't encountered this pathology before, either. "It does tell us something about our killer, though," Kes said. That he had no limits, and he wanted them to know it.

"And this." Harrison held up an evidence bag. "A videocassette. It was under the driver's seat. The foam had been cut to fit it, the tape inserted and tied to the springs with baling twine." He handed it to her. "I've seen something similar in drug-muling vehicles. Do you think the killer missed it?"

"They missed the gun." She opened the bag and turned the cassette over in her hand. It was unlabelled, homemade. "Or they didn't know Olson had it. Make sure Susan can get a VCR set up for tonight's meeting, we'll take a look at it then." She handed it back to him.

"We should be done in a couple hours," Sally said. She was muffled through her mask.

"Perfect, thank you both."

Kes turned her attention on Harrison. "Can I talk to you for a moment?" She led him away from the others. "Are we good?"

"I wasn't sure if I was being punished when you assigned me here." He tried to make it a joke, but she knew he was asking.

"I just wanted you to experience this side of it. I trusted that you'd make sure nothing was missed." She looked back to Doug and Sally, who were absorbed in their work, and stepped in closer to him. "Last night..."

"We don't have to talk about that. I'm good."

But she wasn't convinced. "Hear me out. There are times I'm going to do things, Harrison. If you're ever uncomfortable with it, you do what you have to do. I won't hold it against you. You understand?"

She was giving him a moral out. Once he started following her path, there wouldn't be a place for him to turn around. "Where do you stand now?"

He met her eyes without hesitation. "I want to be a detective."

XXIV.

WHEN KES ENTERED THE STATION, SUSAN LOOKED UP FROM HER DESK. "Captain Puck would like to see you." She appeared worried. "He's...um..."

"Not in a good mood?" Kes offered.

Susan exhaled, relieved she didn't have to say it.

"Thanks for the warning."

Kes carried on to Brownley's room and poked her head in. He was just hanging up the phone.

"How are you doing on that list of schools?"

"Already done, just need to print it." When he smiled, he looked younger and warmer. He and Susan were well-suited, she thought. There was a gentleness between them.

"I would have had it sooner," he said, "but the paperwork on the motel took up most of the afternoon."

"For the meeting is fine."

She made a stop at Chester's desk. He was stooped over his computer, working on the photo she had taken at the bar. She pointed to the suspect. "That's him. Can you enlarge it as best you can and make prints for the meeting?"

"Yes, sir," he said, not catching his slip.

She didn't correct him. In a strange way, she took it as a compliment. She was one of the boys. "Any progress on the tattoo?"

He shuffled through the papers on his desk and grabbed the photo. "I did a quick search. It could be a prison tattoo. A playing card can mean the inmate's a gambler, or they look at life as a gamble."

"And the significance of the ace of clubs?"

"I haven't found anything yet."

"Check prison records," she said. "Nationwide. Our Miss Olson may have been incarcerated at one time. See if Brownley can give you a hand."

He reached for another set of photos that were face-down, but didn't turn them over. "The other tattoo isn't distinct enough to be traced. Standard scroll font. And could be decades old. And the piercings...we could try showing her photo around BDSM clubs, but I don't even know where to look for those. I tried online, but photos just came up of..." He couldn't bring himself to say what he'd seen. "I don't understand it."

"Her sexual preferences may be irrelevant to the case. Focus on the prison records instead for now." She could see his relief. Chester hadn't learned yet how to shield himself.

She grabbed a coffee and added extra sugar, but it was still bitter. She would have preferred a cup of Susan's homemade brew. She found a box of biscuits that were stale but ate one anyway. Then she knocked on Puck's door.

"Come in."

Puck was seated at his desk. His coffee and muffin, likely baked by Susan, were untouched. His hands were on the desk, clasped tightly together, and his body was tight and coiled.

"You wanted to see me?"

"What the hell were you doing at The Brigantine?"

She closed the door behind her. "Following a lead. A man staying there matched our description."

His voice raised. "So you took two police officers and stormed a room?!"

"I take it you got a call from the mayor?" Kes responded calmly.

"Damn rights, I did. She tore a strip off me, wanting to know how I could have approved such a blatant violation. Questioning my oversight. Questioning my capacity as chief. Accusations of police brutality! What do you have to say for yourself?"

Kes considered, then quietly answered. "Was she upset about the conduct of your personnel or by her own indiscretions, sir?"

"Detective, that is not the issue!"

Kes straightened up and her eyes hardened. "I am quite certain that if she had not been in that room, embarrassed that she'd been caught naked, screwing someone other than her husband, she'd be lauding your decisive actions trying to track down a man who's killed three of her constituents. May I return to work now, sir?"

Puck leaned back and pondered her defiance. "Careful, detective, whose feet you tread on." He took a breath. "She was naked?"

"Yes, sir, except for a small, white towel."

"That's going to be a hard image to erase at the next town council meeting." He took a sip of his coffee. "Dismissed."

Kes lowered herself into a chair. She took a moment, then leaned back and found a position that didn't strain her muscles; at least she could bend again. She had slipped into the conference room early to spend time alone with the board. Beyond the door, she could hear the low hum of printers and phones ringing.

She scanned the faces of the victims, the map, the old photographs, and the absence of connecting lines. She opened her phone and pulled up the image of the man at the bar and swiped it open wider, but the pixels blew. She minimized the image and held it up to the faces of the boys in the old black-and-white photo, but couldn't see a match.

She considered the paint colours again—the red, yellow, and green—and looked back at the soccer shorts the boys were wearing. There were stripes: grey, black, and white. She looked at the boy flexing his arm. *Who are you?*

She sat with each of the victims, imagined injecting them with a paralyzer, and wondered how the killer got so close without a fight. No matter the scenarios she played in her head, she always came back to one: the killer walked straight up to the victim, friendly and easy, so as not to spook them. That's how she would have done it. Offering his hand, "Hi." Like he knew them. Maybe he did. He certainly had studied them, their daily patterns, maybe struck up conversations to ingratiate himself. A wolf in sheep's clothing.

The overhead light switched on, and Kes realized the evening had dimmed; she wondered how much time had passed. Chester hesitated in the doorway.

"Sorry, I didn't know you were here already." He had a sheaf of photographs in hand. "I wanted to get things set up."

She checked her watch. Twenty minutes to six. "Of course, come in." In the hall, she could hear the squeak of wheels.

Susan pushed the door open with her bum and hauled in a cart with a TV and VCR. "Oh," she said. "I didn't think anyone would be here yet."

"Come in," Kes said. Susan busied herself hooking up the equipment. Chester offered to give her a hand, but then stood by with the proffered cables not knowing what to do with them.

"Red to red, white to white," Susan said. "In the back." She looked to Kes. "Not often I know more about equipment than a young one."

Brownley entered with a sheaf of papers. "Sorry..."

Kes waved him in.

The door opened again, and it was Harrison with evidence bags from the car search. She waved him in, too. She watched her team busily set up their stations at the table. She loved the camaraderie and ease with which they were working. Susan slipped out, returning with a plate of cheese and crackers, grapes, and bottles of water and said goodnight. At five to six, the men were seated and the room quieted.

"I know you're all aware of this morning's *bust*," Kes said.

Chester laughed and elbowed Brownley, who tried not to smile. "It's okay," she said. She had timed the joke well and the room was appreciative. "But that's as far as it goes."

Brownley became serious. "The mayor's 'friend' checked out. Address was good, driver's license, no priors." He again expressed his remorse to Kes. "Sorry to take us down the wrong path."

"We check every lead and we chase down every possibility. We don't apologize." She paused. "Well, I may have to apologize to a certain local politician, but that's not your worry. And Puck is handling it; he'll keep it away from us. Updates?"

Chester straightened up, "Tele-Link confirmed all three victims had cell plans with the same company. All phones are active, but they're burners and can't be located. It'll take some time to get logs of incoming and outgoing calls. I've applied to the court for a Production Order to serve on Tele-Link—we should have the records end of day tomorrow."

He handed out the photo that Kes took in the bar. "I was able to magnify and clean up the resolution. It's still a little dark, but you can make out the features. Remember, the image is flipped in the mirror."

Each man examined the photo. "Don't recognize him," Brownley said. Nor did the others.

"This is who's been watching you?" Harrison asked.

"Yes." Kes answered the question in his eyes: *Do you think this is who was in your room?* She added it to the board under the photos of the children. "Let's show it around and see if we can get an ID. And Chester, see if his face matches any of these boys'."

Brownley handed out his stapled papers. "I researched schools in the area. There were thirty-six in the county before government cuts consolidated them into seven. A lot of records are missing or lost."

Kes examined the list, which had been augmented with a hand-annotated map detailing the locations. They were colour-coded as active or closed. Brownley was proving to be a diligent tracker. "Any private schools?"

"Just the Montessori, but it only opened a decade or so ago. Doesn't fit the dates you asked for."

"Can we get a list of teachers who taught at these schools in the past thirty years? See if a familiar name pops up?"

Brownley took notes. "I'll look at yearbooks, library archives, class lists, local sports teams, and see if we can find a match. Maybe through the uniforms?"

"Perfect." They were truly becoming a unit, and Kes could see their individual strengths complementing each other.

"We also have a tattoo on Miss Olson with a possible prison connection, Brownley and I are chasing that." He handed out the photo, then hesitated passing out the others, unsure if he should share them.

Kes picked up the pause. "Olson also had piercings on her nipples and labia, and a *Punish me* tattoo across her torso. All that tells us so far is that she enjoyed pain. There's no evidence the murders have a sexual connection, so let's not jump to any conclusions. Anything else before I hand the floor to Harrison?"

All were quiet.

Harrison stood up. "The search of Olson's vehicle revealed a concealed handgun, serial number filed off, and a videotape discovered in a compartment similar to the type used for smuggling drugs." He set the cassette tape on the table and passed out diagrams, indicating where each item was found.

"These show where fingerprints were pulled. Beyond the victim's presumed prints, an additional set was found on the steering wheel, gearshift, mirror, seat pull, and handle. The prints themselves indicate that the fingertips were abraded or burnt off. They won't be able to be matched."

"Crazy shit," Chester muttered.

"The seat was left back by whomever drove it last. The span was longer than the victim's legs. Rear- and side-view mirrors had also been adjusted. Sally estimates the last driver was over six feet."

"Good," Kes said. He hadn't missed a single detail. "Okay. Let's see what's on the tape."

Chester switched off the lights. Harrison slipped the tape into the VCR.

"Old school," said Brownley.

"It certainly is," said Kes. She saw Brownley reach in his pocket to retrieve half a sandwich wrapped in plastic; there was a small note with a heart attached. His face softened and he tucked it in his pocket. She could smell peanut butter. Harrison hit play and the TV hissed white, then flickered. The frame appeared grainy and dark.

"Is there volume?" Kes asked.

Harrison cranked it high, but there was only a garbled hiss. The image fluttered.

"Maybe it was wiped?" Brownley said between mouthfuls.

The camera's exposure brightened, then balanced, and a man's voice off-camera said, "How old?"

The answer was garbled. It was a woman's voice. The camera swept along polished floorboards. Kes grabbed her notebook and started jotting down notes of what she was seeing.

Another man spoke. "Is this on?"

This time they could hear the female clearly reply, "Yes."

The camera tilted up, revealing a cross-like structure. Two boards lashed with rope. The camera slowly swung around from behind to reveal a young boy, gagged and blindfolded, tied to the beams at his ankles and wrists.

Kes sensed Brownley setting his sandwich down. The camera panned down on the boy's naked, hairless body. He was unnaturally still. The light, coming in through a large window nearby, was warm. The entire scene looked staged.

The camera settled on the child's face, obscured by a blindfold and gag. Sandy-brown hair. It panned down again, and a man's hand entered the frame and touched the boy's belly. At the touch, the boy's stomach sucked in and heaved. The hand slid down and the child bucked and struggled. The camera zoomed in tighter on his genitals and then widened frame to include his torso. The hand cupped and rubbed him until the child was erect. Muffled whimpering could be heard.

"Are you getting it?" another man's voice asked. A barber's razor entered frame.

"Not too deep," a woman said.

"Don't block the light," said the cameraman.

"Jesus Christ. I can't—" Brownley's chair scraped as he stood up and turned his back on the TV.

Kes glanced to Chester, whose head was down. Hands clenched and eyes closed. She looked to Harrison, who was staring hard at the image, his eyes gleaming wet.

The blade drew lightly across the boy's torso and blood dripped on to his genitalia, which excited the perpetrator more as he rubbed.

The blade entered frame again and the boy thrashed. The knife pulled back.

"Stop him moving!" A woman's arm entered frame.

"Pause it!" Kes ordered.

Harrison hit stop and Kes walked up to the monitor.

"Rewind. Slowly." The camera tilted back up to the woman's arm entering frame. "There, stop!"

She pointed to the wrist turned slightly upwards. There was a faint black outline. She pulled the photo of the tattoo off the whiteboard and lined it up: the corner of a playing card.

"Play," said Kes.

But the tape didn't start. She looked to Harrison. "Harrison?"

His hand was frozen on the remote, his body shaking. "He looks like Mac at that age," his voice trembled.

"Give it to me." She gently took the remote and stood in front of the monitor, blocking the image. She looked to her men, who had all seen horrors on the job, but, she knew, nothing like this. Their heads were hung low and their shoulders hunched. "Everybody leave the room. I'll watch the rest alone."

"That's not right that you...," Brownley weakly protested.

"Go home," she said. "All of you. That's an order."

They filed out silently and didn't look back.

Kes stood in the darkened room, the light of the TV at her back. She breathed in and out. She swallowed the part of herself that could feel. She stood there until she was numb, then turned around and pressed play.

A howl distorted the sound and the camera tilted up wildly. The boy had slipped his gag and was screaming. The camera shifted to the floor.

"Shut him up," the man said. "I'm not paying for this."

"Be quiet!" the woman's voice shouted.

The camera spun and stayed focused on the floor as the boy continued to shriek. A sound more animal than human.

"Hold him," the woman said. "Shut up! Shut up!"

A man yelped, "He bit me!"

"Open his mouth."

The video cut out and white noise filled the monitor.

Kes turned off the TV. For a long time after, she could hear the boy's scream.

XXV.

KES WAS ON TOP OF THE BED COVERS, FULLY DRESSED; SHE HADN'T EVEN taken off her boots. She hadn't stopped for supper after leaving the station. She barely remembered the drive back to the motel.

She had taken one of her pills and one painkiller, but it wasn't her ribs tormenting her. It was a different pain she wanted to dull.

She looked to her phone, wanting to call the number on display. But she'd be in bed now. If Kes called, it would be for her own selfish need to wrap her arms around her, to smell her hair, and feel the patter of her little heart against her chest. To read bedtime stories where good triumphs over evil and a nightlight shines stars on the ceiling and teddy bears are gathered close. She closed her phone and set it aside. She refused to cry.

All she could do was catch the monsters. She floated on the pills, let them dissolve her mind and heart. Her eyes closed and she walked the crime scenes again.

She tried to visualize the killer's actions, cold and detached. She tried to sit with his rage, but couldn't feel it. The murders were too controlled. She shut herself down more until she felt empty, and that felt truer. She sat in the dark of him. Wrapped herself in his calloused, knotted scars. She conjured each of the victims' faces as she approached them. *They didn't recognize you or didn't think you were a danger, or they would have run. Why did they let their guard down? Had they forgotten you?* She saw them through his calculating eyes. Waiting to strike, luring them closer, his feral heart cloaked. Never betraying his hunger until it was too late.

She stood in front of his bound and drugged victims and looked into their eyes. *You wanted them to see you, didn't you? Wanted them to know who you were. Was there pleasure in that? Revealing yourself?*

No. All she could feel was deadness. And the wild taste of blood bringing down prey.

She tried to feel the body she was in but kept flashing back to the video. She flickered between the man's and boy's skin. Boy and man. Man and boy. Boy-man. She couldn't separate them. *And neither could he*, she realized. She, too, wanted to kill the bastards after seeing the video. What they'd done. She wanted them to fucking pay. No mercy. Slow and painful. Her body twitched. She could hear her dad. A whisper in her brain. *Don't let their blood get in yours.* She shielded herself harder and stepped back in. He's a killer. A serial murderer. *Don't confuse the crimes*, she had to remind herself. But he was a victim, too. They were victims.

She searched her mind for some sense of who he was. *Where are you?* But instead she saw the boy bound, gagged, and blindfolded. She didn't want to go there, but he wanted her to look. Her heart was beating fast and she had broken into a cold sweat. She was inside him, standing before the boy. She reached up and slid the blindfold from the child's eyes—

The phone rang and she jumped. The sun was low and the room was warm.

"Morris," she said. Her mouth was dry.

"Hi, boss. I mean Kes. It's Brownley."

She sat up and rooted her feet to the floor, trying to pull herself back. She was nauseated and the blue room and orange curtains seemed hyper-saturated. Like the videotape's colours.

"Chester, Harrison, and I are heading down to the pub. We wanted to know if you might join us for a beer. Get rid of the day?"

She would.

Her team had chosen a booth near the back of the bar that gave them some privacy. The Ocean View catered more to tourists and she suspected they had chosen it for its anonymity. Copies of old French posters lined the walls, giving the room a pleasant atmosphere. The kitchen was just around the corner and she could see a line cook plating smoked salmon. The waiter had a braided goatee. The place was packed and buzzing with conversation and laughter. She could be in the city, except for the harbour view.

She slipped in beside them with her back to the wall, facing the floor-to-ceiling windows. They had wanted her to have the best seat. A pitcher of beer sat between them. Brownley poured her a drink in a ready glass and slid it over. They raised their pints and drank. Kes drained it. It tasted so good. Brownley poured her another.

They sat in silence. Waiting for her to tell them.

"The video cut out shortly after. There was nothing more revealed about the perpetrators or the victim." She flashed on the image of the boy's screaming mouth and the gag around his neck. She would spare them that horror.

"We know Olson was there. I suspect the other two were involved as well. I believe their victims are our killers."

All of them were holding their beers with clasped hands. The cold glasses offered a comfort and grounding.

"We have our why," she said.

The men nodded, holding the solemnity of this truth. They could have been sitting at a wake.

"They got away with it," Brownley muttered.

"No, they didn't, they were punished," she said. "It doesn't change that we're still looking for their murderers." But it had changed everything. She knew that, and so did they.

"Tonight, let's have a beer or two and some food, my treat," she said.

Let's forget the horror for a short while, is what she was saying. *Let's come back to now, beyond our work, as colleagues. Let's*

*sit and talk for as long as we have to, until we feel able to go home
and sleep. Let's ease back from the pain.*

She waved to the waiter. "Could we have another pitcher,
please, and menus?"

They drank and ate. Told stories about the town and themselves. Laughed about the stupid things people did. They smiled
when talking about their cabins and fishing holes. Brownley
ordered two desserts to split. All agreed they weren't as good as
Susan's. Brownley was the first to bow out. She had noticed him
check his watch.

"Susan will be waiting up for me," he said, sharing for the first
time what everyone already knew. Chester left at the same time;
both offered to split the bill, but Kes refused. It was her treat.

She and Harrison slowly sipped the last finger of their beers.

"I should be going, too," he said, but didn't get up to leave.

"Have you been talking to Mac?" she asked.

"I called him tonight. He's doing good." Harrison finished
his beer. "I miss him though. As much as it drives me crazy listening to his video games and blathering on through the night
to his friends about nothing, I'd give anything to hear him now."
He put down his glass. "But he's good. He's safe. He'll be home.
I'm a lucky man." He stood up. "I'm going to hit the washroom.
Are you going to be good to drive?"

"Yeah, I only had two." The pills were the real issue. The
combination was making her feel warm, like she was floating.
She would walk home, pick up her car tomorrow. It was a beautiful night.

Alone at the table, Kes stared out the window at two fishing trawlers passing through the mouth of the harbour, setting
out to sea. The pub door opened and a group of young people
entered. And behind them was the man from the photo.

She turned and smiled to the waiter. "I'll take the bill,
thanks." As she got out her credit card, she clocked where the
man had sat: opposite her, his back to the window. She paid,
while keeping up a light breezy conversation.

Harrison returned as the waiter was leaving and thanked Kes. "It's what we all needed."

"Don't look. Keep smiling," Kes said. "He's sitting two tables behind us, your right, far window. He just arrived. Blue jacket, grey T-shirt, jeans. Laugh now and tell me you'll see me later."

Harrison laughed and did as she instructed.

"Now, head to the door and we'll wedge him in. I'll be right behind you." Harrison waved a *see you later* and once he was behind the suspect's eyeline, he waited at the door. Kes rummaged in her purse as she left. She looked up and locked eyes with the suspect and smiled. Uncertain, the man looked away and picked up a menu. She glanced to Harrison and both converged.

"Police. I want to talk to you," she said as she approached. He stood up.

"Sit down," Harrison ordered from behind, but he didn't comply.

The man was much shorter than six feet and heavier than the descriptions of the judge at the shooting range.

"We just want to talk," she said. The man took a couple of steps back. He was cornered. "Keep your hands where we can see them."

Harrison reached for his holster. The man was looking for a way out. "Sit down," Kes insisted.

"Okay, okay." He raised his hands to indicate he was acquiescing, took a step towards the chair, then abruptly charged and flipped the table at Kes. Cutlery, plates, and glasses crashed to the floor. Patrons jumped out of their seats. He spun around to escape, but Harrison cut off the doorway exit and two pissed-off patrons blocked the aisle.

"There's nowhere to go," Kes said. The man looked afraid. He wasn't their killer. Their killer wouldn't show fear. Cornered, he took the only way out.

Kes hollered "Stop!" as he plowed through the plate glass window. She ran to the sill to see him scrambling to get up, covered in glass shards. Just as he gained his footing and was stumbling down the slight hill, Harrison tackled him to the ground and quickly restrained him. He looked up to Kes as he put on the cuffs. *We got him*, his eyes said.

But she knew they hadn't. She turned around, noticing the silence. The diner was littered with strewn tables, plates, and food. The floor wet with spilled drinks. Customers were huddled against the walls. A waitress was standing still with a full tray of beers in hand.

"I'm sorry," Kes said to the guests. She looked to the waiter. "I'm sorry. Please call the station to file a damage report." And she walked out.

XXVI.

Mounted in the corner of Holding Cell 1 was a surveillance camera. Kes and Harrison watched the feed from the converted closet down the hall that served as an observation room, a narrow, airless space that had rarely seen use in the station's fifty-year history. It was small, but Kes was fine so long as she was mentally prepared and didn't have to stay any longer than necessary. Still, she told Harrison to keep the door open.

The station only had two cells, side by side, used primarily as drunk tanks or temporary holding until suspects could be transferred to the city. They resembled cages, with steel bars on three sides, and were original to the building. Each had a bench that served as a cot, and a toilet and sink bolted to the back wall.

The quality on the monitor was poor but adequate. Their suspect couldn't sit still. He'd pace and sit. Pace and sit. When he sat, a leg bounced nervously. Once the medics cleared him of life-threatening injuries, Kes had allowed them to administer taped sutures for the cuts and scrapes only, no painkillers.

"Let him sit. No water," Kes said. "We'll talk to him in the morning."

"Night shift will look in on him every twenty minutes," said Harrison.

"Nobody sees him before we do." She was weary. Her muscles and ribs ached. Her eyes were dry. "I'm going to get some sleep. You should, too."

"I'd like to be here when you talk to him."

"Oh-seven-hundred," she said. "Leave your report until the morning. I'll call Puck tonight." Kes could see his tiredness, too.

She noticed small cuts on his forearm and hands. "Did you get those checked out?"

"I'm good, I'll dress them at home." He stared back at the monitor, unwilling to leave. She knew his question before he asked. Heard his guarded hope.

"Is it him?"

She watched the suspect get up and pace the room again.

"No." This one wasn't going to be that easy.

It was a long conversation with Puck. Kes had woken him. He was silent as she described the videotape. Cursed when she told him about the bar. Tore into her for taking risks in a public place. Berated her for not waiting until the suspect was outside to take him down, and gave her hell for not calling for backup. He spoke fast and out of breath as he cited all the ways things could have gone wrong. What if he'd had a weapon, had taken a hostage, had opened fire? The list went on, until he finally exhausted his anger.

She stayed on the line, listening to him breathe.

"What time?" he asked.

"Oh-seven-hundred," she said, and Puck hung up.

Kes laid back on the bed and that was the last she remembered. When she woke, she was grateful she couldn't recall the nightmares.

Puck and Kes walked down the hall in silence to the interview room. He was still upset with her. Their morning briefing had been professional, but distant. He would join her in the interrogation, which felt like a slight, like he didn't trust her not to do something rash. It was agreed she would take the lead, so she was surprised when he said "Ready?" and flung the door open so hard it smashed into the wall. The suspect's head, resting on the table, snapped up. His eyes were red and his lips dry. The cuts looked sore.

Kes shut the door behind her.

Puck strode up to the man and stood over him but didn't speak. *Pure intimidation.* The man leaned back, and Puck put his hands on the table and leaned in. The man breathed uneasily and his eyes shifted to Kes.

Puck looked at the man's wounds. "Those look sore," he said, and grabbed the man's hand and squeezed. He squirmed and winced in pain.

"Now here's what you're going to do. Detective Morris is going to ask you questions. You're going to answer them. If I think you're not telling the truth, I'm going to bloody well hurt you. Got it?"

The man nodded and Puck squeezed once more, causing him to curl into a whimper. "All yours," he said.

Kes had never seen this side of the captain. She knew Harrison was watching through the two-way mirror. She sat on the chair across from the suspect. "Are you thirsty?"

He licked his lips and nodded. She looked to Puck, who wasn't impressed but followed her lead. He stepped out to get the water.

Kes said nothing. She just stared, which made him fidget. Searching for somewhere else to look. Puck returned with a paper cup, and the man flinched when he set it close to his bandaged hands.

"Go ahead," Kes said. He sucked back the drink.

"Better?" She leaned forward, elbows resting on her knees.

"What's your name?"

"Billy."

"Billy what."

"Billy Cochrane."

"Where do you live?"

"I've got an old boat down the river I'm fixing up. I stay on that."

"What do you do, Billy Cochrane?"

"This and that. Recycle. Buy and sell."

"If I start digging, will I find a rap sheet of stolen goods?"

He hesitated. "There might have been some misunderstandings."

"It's good you're being honest with me, Billy," she said. He wasn't smart; he appeared to be what he was: a scammer and a thief. "Why were you following me?"

"I got paid," he said.

"By whom?"

"I don't know."

Puck stepped closer. "'I don't know'?"

"A guy approached me one day when I was..." He chose his words carefully. "...salvaging some parts and offered me a lot of money to just watch you. Told me where you were staying. Said to follow you and don't get caught." He fingers rubbed the table like he was soothing himself or remembering his lines. "Figured you were an ex he wanted to fuck with. Paid cash up front. Five hundred bucks a day for five days. I wasn't supposed to do nothing, not touch you, just watch. Real easy money. He said he'd know if I fucked up."

"What did the person who hired you look like?"

"Tall, wore sunglasses. Drove a green car, kinda beat up. I asked him if he was interested in selling it."

"Where was he from?"

"He seemed local to me. Knew the area, you know. But I never seen him before." Billy unrolled the rim of the paper cup as he talked.

"When were you going to meet up again?"

"There was no talk of that. It was like a done deal. I needed to fix the boat engine and what he paid was going to cover that. Get her back on the water. Didn't seem like it was going to hurt nobody."

"Why did you ransack my room?"

Puck looked at her. This was the first he was hearing about it.

"No way, I didn't do that! I just watched. Followed you to

dinner, made sure you noticed, and then left. That was my job. That's it. I never went in nobody's room, swears to Jesus."

"Okay, Billy. We're going to keep you a bit longer. Check out your story. If I don't see any problems, we'll send you home. I'll get someone to bring you a coffee and a muffin. That sound good to you?"

"Yeah."

Kes headed for the door. Puck put his hand on Billy's shoulder and pressed down. Billy groaned. "Don't you ever follow one of my crew again. You understand?"

"Yes," he moaned.

"I didn't hear that. What was that?"

"Yes, sir."

Puck walked past Kes and out the door.

"What do you think?" Puck asked her out in the hallway. "You believe him?" Whatever anger or distance she'd read from him was gone. It had been a performance. She had underestimated him.

"He's not our murderer. But I'm not ready to cross him off the list. I'd like to put a tail on him. See where he goes."

Puck sighed. "We don't have the personnel or budget for stakeouts, Kes. This isn't the city."

Harrison joined them from the observation room. "My office," Puck said to Kes. And to Harrison, "Not you." Kes followed the captain.

"Shut the door."

Kes remained standing and waited for Puck to settle behind his desk.

He could see her preparing her argument and stopped her. "I'll give you Sally and Doug for forty-eight hours. Tell me what you're thinking."

"Billy was paid for five days in advance, which means the killers plan to be around at least that long. He's been tailing me for three days. They're going to strike again. It's not over."

"Jesus." Puck held his head in hands. She felt bad for him.

His gentle, well-earned ride to retirement was careening over a cliff. "Do we have any leads?"

"The tape, the photos...we have to find out who these boys are and where the original crimes happened. It happened somewhere *here*, sir."

"I can't believe it." His view of his idyllic town was collapsing. "I'm going to have to release something to the press, warn the public. The mayor's going to be all over me. This is going to have an impact on tourist season. The town's reputation. And the damage at the bar last night..."

"I'll take the blame," Kes said.

"No, you won't." He sat up straight. "It's what had to be done. And what will be done. It's not your concern." He looked at the stitches on her cheek and the bruise under her eye. It was obvious she was still favouring one side. "Someone tossed your room?"

"It wasn't a big deal. I didn't want to bother you with something that had no impact on the case."

She could feel his disappointment in her deflection.

"You're not solo here, Kes," he said. "You're working under me and you are ultimately my responsibility." He reached in his desk and slid a small revolver and holster towards her. "You will carry this from now on. Understood?"

"Yes, sir."

She picked up the weapon and turned to leave.

"Kes." Puck stopped her. "I'm glad to have you here."

XXVII.

Her team was waiting when Kes entered the conference room.

"You all right?" Harrison asked.

"Yep. All good." She shifted to ease the holster from pressing against her ribs. She looked to her team. "Did Harrison update you on what transpired last night, and our interview?"

"We're up to speed," Brownley said.

"Good. Puck has given us a forty-eight-hour detail to follow Billy Cochrane once he's released. Which, if I'm right, is the same amount of time we have before the next murder. They're not finished yet, I'm certain of it. We need a break in these cases."

Chester spoke first: "I talked to Child Trafficking. They have very little on crimes from the late eighties, early nineties. Most tapes went underground or were destroyed, or simply deteriorated. Victims rarely came forward then. I'll pull a tape transfer and they'll cross-check for anything they have, but they're not hopeful."

He shifted in his seat and seemed to steel himself before he spoke again. "There's a market for this type of video that will pay big money. The more grotesque, the higher the price. Boy and boy. Boy and man. Boy and animal. All the way up to mutilation, castration..." Chester faltered, but quickly recovered. "The sicker the atrocity, the higher the price. That place we saw in the video could have been a snuff factory for this kind of supply."

"Or the tapes were a side business," Brownley suggested. "And the real money was in selling the victims by the hour for whatever horror these sick bastards could conceive." He looked to Kes. "Do you really think this was happening here in this town? Our town? Kids were…" He couldn't carry on.

"I do," said Kes. She could feel the collective weight of guilt in the room. Regardless if it was before their time, the police had failed. "Chester, go back through old files—see if there were any allegations, improprieties, or complaints of sexual misconduct involving minors. We know these people had access to children. They had privacy. Authority. Control. There were multiple perpetrators involved. It was organized. We know our victims are connected somehow."

She turned to the photos on the board. "We can presume they were part of a ring." She pulled down the photo of the boys' soccer team. "We're looking for a school," she said. "Not public, maybe private. Or a detention centre or orphanage…lost kids. A place that could operate without scrutiny. With impunity. Our killers come from there. It's where they're returning." She turned to her men. "We have to find it and we have to find it now."

The team spent the afternoon huddled around computers and sifting through file cabinets. Brownley went to the library and returned with stacks of archival history books about the area. Kes and Harrison checked over the list of schools that had been closed over the recent decades. Most were small rural schools that the locals had fought to keep open, but to no avail. None struck Kes as having the right location or student profile to fit their criteria. Most were too public or too small or had extensive parental involvement.

Chester got a hit on a Missy Olson. Served time out west when she was twenty-seven years old. Did five months for running a gambling book on minor sports. Back in the same jail two years later; time served and the record expunged.

Brownley got an evaluation back on the two undamaged stamps found at Doc's house. They were misprints of the St. Lawrence Seaway. The centre was inverted. It was estimated that only four hundred such stamps were printed, so extremely rare. Most were in the hands of private collectors and worth about ten thousand dollars apiece. Their dead man, who'd lived like a pauper, had money to invest.

They had emptied Susan's coffee pots twice and eaten her lunch offerings without tasting them. They were quiet and focused, their eyes dry from perusing computer screens and mouldy books.

On the occasions when Kes looked up over her team's bowed heads, she'd see Puck in his office watching them, or on his phone in forceful discussions.

They were heading into their fifth straight hour when Chester called them over. "I think I have something," he said.

He'd been double-checking schools and found mention of one missing from all the official lists. "A government school that burned down in the late nineties. It was about thirty kilometres from town."

"Shit. I remember hearing about that place...to help home-less kids or something?" Brownley said. "Burned down about five years before I came here."

"I remember that," Harrison said. "I was just a kid then, but I remember people talking about a fire."

Chester did a deeper web search. "There's a story about the fire in the local paper, but it's vague. People didn't seem to know much about the place. It was some sort of federal-run program. Took in kids from across the country who were either runaways or orphans." He pulled up an article. "This says it had been an old fishing lodge for the wealthy. The Mid River runs behind it, a famous salmon river in its day. Now you'd be lucky to find a brown trout in it. It's a secluded spot. Then it became a school or reformatory, the Holy Cross School for Boys."

"It was a religious-based operation?" Kes looked to the sil-ver crosses displayed on the board.

"I don't think so. Maybe they used the name to make people think they were religious. Or to get a tax deduction."

"Can you pinpoint its location, Chester?"

"Off Highway 3; I can track it through aerials and old maps."

Kes grabbed her coat. "Harrison, you're with me. Chester, we're going to need a list of the teachers and students who attended the school. Check with the federal archives to get everything on the place. Brownley, I want you to go Doc's house. There are stacks of papers and magazines there...maybe there's a brochure or yearbook, anything at all about the school. And Brownley, keep checking in with the detail on Billy." She took a deep breath. "This is where it began," she said. "This is our break, gentlemen."

As her team dispersed, Kes stopped in front of the board and looked at the photo of the young boys. Somewhere in those faces were the killers.

She glanced to the morgue photos and suppressed her revulsion. *They're the victims*, she told herself. But her heart snarled.

XXVIII.

THEY TURNED LEFT OFF THE HIGHWAY ONTO A BRIDGE THAT TOOK THEM over the river. Harrison hit a pothole and his truck took the impact hard. Kes tensed her abdomen to absorb the shock of pain.

Flocks of songbirds landed in the trees beside the road. *Coming home*, she thought. It always mystified her how birds could navigate thousands of miles to return to the same spot every year. In comparison, humans were simple creatures.

"That was five kilometres. After a small bridge, we should see a dirt road on our left." Harrison was glued to his GPS and missing the beauty of the birds. They drove over an old wooden-planked bridge. "It has to be around here." He slowed.

They saw a gravel road off to the left and pulled in. It was overgrown with tall grass that brushed against the undercarriage of the truck. As they neared the river, the trees changed to mostly hemlock and willow that had grown to impressive heights. The road ended in a large field. Harrison shut off the truck. Kes breathed in the sweet smell of new growth. Birds trilled and she could hear the roar of the river.

They walked the area and found the remains of a blackened concrete foundation wall that poked above the weedy grass. A few piles of bricks lay about the site. Dense woods surrounded the clearing. Twenty feet up, on some of the tree trunks, she could see evidence of scorching and dead limbs. The location was hidden and remote.

Kes followed the sound of the river to the edge of the woods. The bush was dense, and she wandered along the natural barrier looking for an opening through the tangle of limbs to glimpse the water. She could see light, and ducked under the branches into a small clearing overlooking the churning river, surging with spring runoff.

She stopped. Ahead were five crude wooden crosses made from weathered, salvaged boards nailed together. No names or ornamentation. She moved towards them, looking for signs of burial. But the ground was level. She didn't have the uneasy sense of bones beneath her feet.

A large, gnarled apple tree was blossoming nearby. She walked towards it. Beneath it were three smaller crosses set apart from the others. Facing the river. Moss and weather had eroded their surfaces. She ran her fingers over the wood and could feel faint indents. The names and dates lost. She looked back to the other markers. They faced the school. She checked for impressions of graves, but it was undisturbed, except for what looked like a deer trail bruising the grass. Yet she could feel it. This place held the eerie stillness of death.

She returned to the field. Harrison was on his knees, pulling at weeds along the crumbled foundation wall. The burial ground was no more than a hundred metres from what would have been the school.

She joined Harrison. "Find something?"

He had scraped away the soil, exposing a metal bar. He tugged and yanked and extracted a large metal cross, its arms bowed from heat.

"There's a cemetery through that bush," Kes said. "Eight crosses, no names. We need to find out everything about this place." They stood in the sadness of it all. When she started to feel the pain, she stepped away. "I want to know what happened to the children who were here."

While Harrison was on the phone updating Puck, Kes walked the perimeter of the clearing following the downed, rusted fencing and barbed and razored wire that encircled the school's rubble. She touched a strand and her skin crawled. She reached into her coat pocket and retrieved the newspaper clipping Chester had found.

HOLY CROSS SCHOOL FOR BOYS
DESTROYED BY FIRE

A former fishing lodge and surrounding woods were consumed by flames on Friday night as local brigades from three counties fought to contain the blaze. Firefighters found a group of young boys huddled and hiding in the woods nearby, barely clothed, some suffering from smoke inhalation. The boys say they were asleep when the fire started. Firefighters battled through the night and most of Saturday, but the building couldn't be saved. Recovery of bodies is underway.

She held up the article with its grainy black-and-white photo, captioned *Opening of Holy Cross School for Boys*, and lined it up with the foundation. The school of brick and wood resurrected in her mind. A large metal cross hung above the door. She searched the empty windows for faces.

XXIX.

KES KNOCKED ON THE SCREEN DOOR OF THE OLD SALTBOX HOUSE. IT WAS beautifully situated on a low cliff that had a view of the town across the bay. Seemed a bit much for a retired school board director. Brownley had called to tell them he'd found the name of the district superintendent during the time of the fire: John Meisner.

An elderly man opened the door.

"Mr. Meisner?"

"Yes?"

"I'm Detective Morris and this is Officer Harrison. We understand you were the director for the school board throughout much of the nineties and we're hoping to ask you some questions about the Holy Cross School for Boys."

His gaze turned inward, like he was being pulled back into a time he didn't want to remember. "That wasn't under my jurisdiction," he said. "That was a federal operation, and I wouldn't call it a school."

"What do you mean?"

"It's a sad story."

"We're just hoping to talk to someone who can tell us about it."

"Come in," he said, leaving the door open. Kes and Harrison followed.

The house was tidy and well-arranged, elegant in its simple design. In the living room, a fire was burning in the beachstone fireplace. The walls were lined with shelves of books and mineral samples.

"Tea?" he offered.

"No thank you," Kes answered for both of them.

"I would like one," Mr. Meisner said, and left them waiting. They stood before the wall of windows overlooking the peninsula. She could see bee hives on the lawn.

He returned with a teacup, a small pot of honey, and a plate of cookies. He sat down on a soft, worn chair.

"You have a beautiful home," Kes said. It had a peacefulness that made her want to stay.

"Thank you." He waved for them to sit.

"You're a beekeeper?"

"Indeed." He dolloped a spoonful of honey into his cup. "These are hard-working and amusing hives that I tend. I often sit out back and watch them foraging. Did you know that a bee will visit up to one hundred flowers in an outing? Imagine that."

"Hard to imagine." Kes would like to sit with him and watch the bees.

He stirred his tea and set the spoon down. "I haven't heard the name of that place in many, many years."

"You said it didn't fall under your purview?" Kes said. Harrison pulled his notebook out and sat with his pen poised.

"It was federally mandated, so I had no say in its curriculum or governance. It was apparently a home for troubled boys. Fully government funded in a period when the Feds were sinking money into a variety of private projects here. Not one of them successful." Kes could hear his contempt. "It was quite a facility, though. Some political connections were at play to invest that much money in the backwoods." He sipped his tea and offered them a cookie, which they refused.

"Were you ever there?" Kes asked.

"Once." He dipped a cookie in his tea. "They had an open house when they renovated the buildings. A number of us were invited to celebrate the good work the government had done in our region. A big fluffy photo opportunity. But as per most make-work projects, only one local person was employed, a janitor by the name of Rodger 'Pickle' Henry. It was hard not to be jealous of the place. It had everything, right on the river."

He looked to the expansive view out his window. "The staff lived in an old fishing lodge and the boys were housed in an addition that was constructed to mirror the camp. A bunkhouse/dormitory style at the back, and then classrooms, common room, a great-room eating area, gymnasium, and an art room with massive windows." He looked to his hives. "Back then, we were all fighting to keep our paltry budgets and our community schools open, but we lost most of those battles. So, this place was quite a slap in the face to the local schools." He smiled apologetically and set down his tea. "But you're not here for that."

This was a man who had cared. "Did you meet any of the teachers or students during your visit?"

"No, the students and teachers hadn't arrived yet." Mr. Meisner had a warm, deep voice that reminded Kes of her father's. "Only the director was there that day."

"Do you remember his name?"

"He was introduced as the *Gov'nor*. That's how it was pronounced. I can't remember if I ever heard his actual name, but I clearly recall not liking the man. Tall with thin lips and eyes that never seemed to blink. Hawk-like. I didn't trust him."

She could hear Harrison's pen scratching down notes.

"And you never saw the boys?"

"No. We reached out over the years to see if the children would like to participate in the local school tournaments, baseball or soccer and whatnot, but we were always turned away. They had their own programs, we were told."

"Do you remember the fire?"

He sighed. "You don't forget something like that. I was sitting in this chair when I heard the news. A tragedy of the highest magnitude for a teacher, the loss of students in your care. How do you live with that? They didn't even have proper funerals for them as far as I know."

"Do you know what happened to the other children?"

He shrugged. "Sent back to wherever they came from, or to other institutions. Some ran away or escaped. At least that's what I heard."

"And the teachers?"

"Not a clue. Poof, they just disappeared. I never heard hide nor hair of them afterwards. Certainly not one applied for a teaching position with us." Kes could see he was drained. "I wish I could tell you more. I just don't know much. They kept apart."

"You've been very helpful, thank you." Kes rose to leave and the men stood.

"Just a moment, Detective." Meisner retrieved a small container from his pocket and offered it to her. "A honey balm to lessen the scarring." He touched his cheek.

"Thank you," she said, accepting his gift. She was touched by this small act of kindness, and for a moment he had cracked through the tough facade that let her do her job and made her feel like a visitor instead.

"You're welcome back any time to watch the bees and try some of the nectar of their labour," he said as he led them to the door. Kes wondered how he had read her so well.

Just as they stepped outside, he said, "It was an institution." His voice dropped low and sombre. "The day I was there, they were erecting 'safety fences'—that's what they called them—ten feet high around the property. Barbed wire. It was a cage. There was nothing holy about that place."

Kes left the old man's house feeling better than when she'd gone in. The warmth of the home he had created was palpable, but she couldn't imagine a life of such contentment for herself. It seemed she could only watch it though windows. Harrison was quiet on the drive back. He'd been quiet all day. They pulled into the station and parked.

"You okay?" she asked.

He closed his eyes for a second. "I keep thinking of Mac.

If someone ever touched him, I'd kill them." He looked at her, his eyes hard. "I would. We're chasing victims, Kes. Where's the justice in that?"

She corrected him. "We're chasing murderers and trying to stop them before they strike again."

"That's what we tell ourselves." Harrison got out of the truck and didn't wait for her. She watched him enter the station.

Her words had sounded hollow even to her. *The victims are the killers,* she told herself. *Judge and executioner. They're circumventing justice. What justice?* The bastards had gotten away with it. How many other victims were there? She tried to sense her father's guidance, but felt nothing.

She reached in her coat pocket for her pills. There were six painkillers left. She took one. She would stop taking them all the moment she finished the case. She always did.

XXX.

THEIR EVENING MEETING WAS SUBDUED, EVEN THOUGH THE SEARCH WAS narrowing its focus. There was every indication that the killers had been students at the Holy Cross School for Boys; that the victims were part of a ring that abused their wards; that there were others in charge who must have known.

Any hope of gaining information from the janitor who had worked there ended with a quick search and the discovery of an obituary listing for the man known as Henry "Pickle." He'd died of cancer eight months previously at the Pine Bluffs Nursing Home. No relatives, no belongings. Whatever he knew died with him.

Which left them with the man known as the Gov'nor. This was who they needed to find. Priority was given to tracking down names and locations of past students and teachers and accessing all available files about the school. Facts were shared. Lists of actions made. But the room felt heavy and uninspired. Brownley articulated what was eating at them all.

"Maybe we just let them finish what they started."

This had gone far enough. Kes stood up. "So what, we just look away? That's what you want to do? Become an accessory to the next murder? Because there *will* be another murder. Let them get their personal justice?" She tried to silence the voice shouting back *yes.* "Vengeance can feel like justice. It would feel good, wouldn't it? Retribution for all they endured. All we have to do is walk away...give them the time they need, right?"

The men were avoiding eye contact. Kes turned to the board and started tearing down the photos, maps, everything.

"Why not? Chester, you can go back to fishing. Brownley, you can have a nice supper with Susan. Puck can go back to his golf game, and Harrison can go to his son. It's perfect." She tossed the photos on the table.

"Box them up. Eye for an eye. Let it rage! Let everyone take vengeance. No more courts, no more hours and weeks and years trudging through the mire and shit of life. We go home. We let the blood spill. Fuck it all!"

She slammed the evidence boxes on the table. The pill had loosened a white rage inside. She wasn't angry at them. Hell, she understood their moral conflict. The rage was with herself, because at her darkest core, she wanted to walk away, too. But she couldn't.

It's a thin line that separates us from them. Her father's words. She took a breath. "It's not my job to judge. My job is to track and bring criminals to justice. Regardless of whatever horror was inflicted on them. One or more of these boys became cold-blooded murderers. Psychopaths with no remorse, willing to use other innocent boys to pull the trigger. We have no idea how far their vengeance can reach. How, in their twisted child's minds, the entire town could be guilty. And maybe they were! Nobody knew? Bullshit."

Kes reined herself in until she could feel only her own heartbeat. She spoke quietly. "If you can't do this job anymore, request to be removed from the case. No questions asked. I'll pass on recommendations." She looked to her men. "But I can't stop. I won't."

The room was quiet. Overhead, a fluorescent light flickered. Brownley gathered up the photos and began arranging them back onto the board. Chester put up the maps, and Harrison collected the strewn paperwork.

"See you tomorrow," Brownley said on his way out the door.

"I'll be in early," Chester said.

Harrison didn't say anything, but nodded goodnight, and shut the door behind him.

The halibut arrived sizzling in a small pool of butter and chopped parsley, along with a cold beer. Kes was ravenous. She cut into the fish and was about to take her first bite when a man leaned against the bar.

"Anything you can tell me about the murders over the last few days, Detective?" He had a notepad and pencil in hand.

"I'm eating. Talk to my captain."

"This won't take much of your time. I just want—"

She set her fork down. "I don't care what you want. I've had a long day. I want a moment alone to eat my dinner, drink my beer, and go to sleep."

"C'mon, Detective, one statement. The public has a right to know if we have a serial killer in town...is that what we have?"

Kes's hands were clenched and her back was quivering. It was taking every bit of her energy not to punch this asshole in the face.

"I've asked you nicely to go away," she said. Her lips were tight.

"One word: do we have a serial killer? Yes or no, and I'll leave you alone. Otherwise, maybe I'll pull up a seat and order a beer. I like to review my notes out loud, you could nod if—" A large, weathered hand clamped down on the man's shoulder and squeezed hard.

"What the hell?" He was spun away from Kes.

"The lady is eating her dinner. You heard her say she's had a long day. Bugger off." It was Captain Phil from the lobster boat. He shoved the reporter off his stool. "Your mother raised you better than this, Tommy. Now fuck off."

"It's my job—"

The captain stepped in closer. His girth and height overpowered the man. "Surely you have another major story to chase about cars being broken into."

"I'm a proper journalist, Phil."

"Captain," he corrected him. "I remember when you were a little wharf-rat, Tommy, scrounging for bait and busting into cars for loose change—so don't you be pulling your *I'm-something-now* shit with me. Now get."

The reporter grabbed his pencil and scurried off. Captain Phil smiled at her. "He's a peckerwood. Ambitious, but an okay kid. You eat, I'll be back with a beer when you're done. If that's okay?"

Kes smiled. "I'd like that."

She finished her fish and toyed with the salad. She wasn't as hungry as she'd thought. A fresh mug of beer slid along the counter in front of her.

"Next time, try the daily special. Lobster sandwich." Captain Phil winked. "I hear the lobster's good."

She played along, "Any I've met before?"

"Well, I'd say most of those have been ate already." He held out his mug and she clinked his glass.

"Thanks for earlier. Saved me from getting myself into more trouble."

"Nothin' to it." He took a swig and reached into his pocket. "Look, we went out to the pen yesterday and found this. Was going to bring it over to the station, but fishing was too good." He held out a small piece of colourful fabric and laid it between them. "It was snagged in the wire. Don't know if it means anything, but in case..."

Kes picked up the cloth. It looked like the stripe from a uniform. Red, green, and gold. *School colours.*

"That was a beastly day," the captain said. "I don't know how you can look at that ugliness all the time."

"Some days are better than others," she admitted. He looked deep in her eyes, until she looked away. She wasn't used to someone probing her.

The captain finished his drink in one draw, set his mug down, and looked around the bar. "You know, it's a good feeling to see all these folks enjoying what you harvested for them. Fishermen rarely get to see that nowadays. Everything you catch is loaded onto a plane and taken somewhere else. You get paid, but you don't get to see the reward. It's hard some days, toiling away in storms, cold and dark, you can forget why you're out there. What took you there in the first place." Kes wasn't sure whether he was talking about himself or her.

He got up to leave and swayed slightly. Kes wondered if it was from too much beer or the perpetual rock of the sea in him.

"When you need it, you should come out on the boat. The ocean's a good place to forget. I hope you catch what you're after." He took his leave.

She felt emotional and knew she was overtired and worried about her team. They were all giving up part of themselves for this job. She checked her phone. It was too late to call her. She considered ordering another beer.

There's honour in this job—finding the truth, no matter how hard, her father would say. *Don't lose that. It takes courage.* He'd tell her that late in the night, when his words were slurred from too many drinks.

Rather than going straight to the motel for much needed sleep, Kes aimlessly drove the town's empty streets for hours. Driving always helped her think. The crime scenes flitted in and out of her mind and settled on Doc's house. She turned around and headed towards Hobson Road. She felt a nagging worry that she had missed something. Something fleeting that she had noticed and dismissed.

She parked in front of the dark house, grabbed the flashlight from her glove compartment, and crossed the police tape. The front door was locked, but she remembered an old wooden side door off the kitchen that had looked original to the house. One sharp tug and it opened. The same caustic smell confronted her.

The wind had picked up and branches rubbed against the shingles. Brownley had returned to the scene earlier to search for any papers or books that could link Doc to the Holy Cross School, but to no avail. Still, she couldn't shake the feeling that there was something here. She panned her flashlight across the toppled piles of magazines and newspapers and headed to the cubby under the stairs.

She focused her beam on the hardened layers of paint etched with the outlines of the stamp books that were now in evidence. *Red, green, and yellow.* The same colours as the swatch Captain Phil found. She stepped back into the living room and listened to the stillness of night. She retraced her steps in her mind and went upstairs.

The staircase creaked loudly underfoot. She went directly to the bedroom. Now a dead man's room. It felt like it had always been lonely. One pillow. One chair. No softness or colour anywhere. She checked the closet again. Nothing on the shelf, nothing on the floor, no false walls. She turned off her flashlight and stood in the dark, playing back the last time she was there. There had been a phone call. She reached for the clothes in the closet and ran her fingers over the fabric. And stopped.

She switched on her flashlight and pushed away the thrift-store clothes until her fingers rested on the shoulder of a fine-quality, worsted wool suit coat. The lining was a rich, silken fabric. She ran her fingers down the lapel, noting the fine stitching. She checked the pockets and felt an envelope.

It was linen. The card inside was printed on quality paper stock. Elegant and simple design. She opened it. It was an invitation to a private dinner, members only. Entertainment to be provided. RSVP to be sent to Martha and Harold Nichols. Holy Cross School for Boys. The event was twenty-five years ago. She reached into her pocket for the newspaper clipping and checked the date of the fire. Three days before the event.

She looked at the invitation again. *Martha and Harold.*

"Gov'nor," she said. "I've found you." She twigged at the memory of the female's voice on the tape and felt a certainty in her gut. "It was you."

She checked her phone, 04:00, and called Puck.

XXXI.

KES KNOCKED ON THE GLASS QUARTER PANEL OF THE NIGHT ENTRANCE. She could see the night-duty officer sound asleep, his head resting on folded arms. "You've got to be fucking kidding me." She spotted a wooden wedge used to prop the door open and thumped it against the casing repeatedly. The officer sat up abruptly, straightening his uniform and brushing back his hair.

"Open the door!" Kes held her badge up and the officer buzzed her in.

She barged into the station and tossed the wedge on the floor. "Is this how you keep watch? What's your name?"

"Sergeant Spenser. They call me Spence." He was trying desperately to look sharp and awake.

"Get Brownley, Chester, and Harrison on the phone. I want them in here now."

"Yes, ma'am."

"And I need an address for a Martha and Harold Nichols. Search within a fifty-kilometre radius, go further if you can't locate them. Try Nicholson if you don't get a hit. Get Chester on it if you can't manage. And tell them to suit up when they arrive."

She headed to the conference room.

"Ma'am...?"

What did he not understand about the urgency of the situation? "What?"

"A Martha and Harry Nicholson live next door to my mother," the officer said. "Not quite the same name...but they're in their seventies."

A simple name change. The age was right. It was them. It had to be them. They hadn't left their hunting ground. "What's the area like?" she asked.

"Cottage country, big lots, back off the main roads. Private."

"Pull up what you can on them and a map of the area. Put a call into them."

"It's not even 04:30."

"Do it."

Kes walked into the conference room and flicked on the overhead light. She pulled the fabric swatch from her pocket and held it up against the photo of the boys. She took out her phone, switched it to black-and-white mode. It was definitely a match.

She rearranged the photos, leaving an empty row at the top, where she wrote *Martha and Harold Nichols* and drew connecting lines to the deceased victims. Above their names, she placed the photos of the boys' soccer team and the young boy flexing his bicep.

"We're not far behind you now," she said.

Spence knocked on the door and poked his head in. "No answer at the Nicholsons'."

As he turned, Kes saw his shuffling limp. He noticed her gaze. "Got clipped at a traffic stop. Puck kept me on. Sorry about earlier. Won't happen again."

"I know it won't." She was reminded how quickly life could change.

"Your team's on the way." He shut the door and Kes could hear his foot dragging down the hall.

Harrison's truck slid around another tight turn, gravel spitting up from the tires. She checked the side view. Chester and Brownley were close behind in an unmarked car. She had ordered no sirens. They were barrelling down a labyrinth of graded dirt roads, leading past extravagant gated vacation homes. Kes could see it had once been comprised of local family cottages cobbled together with plywood and lumber scraps, of which only a few remained.

They pulled onto the road leading to Osprey Lake just as the sun was peeking over the trees. The lake was dead calm, mirroring the treeline on the far side.

The narrow driveway was long and wended through a canopy of trees. Private. Eight acres with a few hundred feet of waterfront. At the end of the driveway was a modern glass-and-concrete single-storey house that didn't try to fit in with its surroundings. Aerial surveys had confirmed there was only one road into the property.

The team took their positions: Chester and Brownley circled around back. Kes and Harrison took the front. They approached with weapons drawn. The birds were singing and the dawn smelled sweet with dew. Kes listened for activity inside, but all she could hear was the squawk of morning crows.

Harrison gently pushed down on the door handle. The door creaked open, revealing a short entryway with one massive granite step. It wasn't unusual for people in these parts to leave their doors unlocked.

Kes took the lead and Harrison covered her. She stepped forward and lowered her gun. Behind her, Harrison whispered, "Kes..." She held up her hand, signalling for him to wait, and stepped out of his sightline.

Quietly, he heard her say, "Clear." Not letting down his guard, Harrison rounded the corner. It was a large living room with a vaulted ceiling above a wall of windows overlooking the lake, creating the illusion of being outside.

"Don't touch anything." She glanced to Harrison's ashen face. "Radio the others to stay outside. Get Brownley to call it in to Puck. Get Chester to notify the medical examiner and then set up a perimeter."

"Shouldn't we search the rest of the house?"

"They're not here," she said and holstered her weapon.

Harrison was still staring straight ahead. Gun drawn. His finger on the trigger.

"Put your weapon away," she gently said. "Go get things started. Tell the others I need ten minutes alone before they come in."

He left, and she could hear the chatter of radio communication outside. Brownley stepped up to the window and placed his hand on the glass to peer in. He quickly stepped back, waving Chester away.

She put on her gloves and moved towards the man hanging from his ankles from the main ceiling beam.

His hands were tied and dangling down. His wrists had been slashed following the course of the arteries. He was naked, and his skin had taken on a blueish pallor. Droplets of blood were still slowly dripping from his wrists that were tethered to the floor. She remembered that a human body held over a gallon of blood. All of which had drained.

She looked to the woman lying beneath him. Her head was secured by leather straps nailed into the floorboards. Blocks of wood on either side ensured that she couldn't move. She was positioned with her mouth directly beneath the man's hands. Her nostrils and mouth were full of his blood. A slow, torturous drowning.

Her eyes were open, still wide with terror. Kes looked at her naked body. Her arms were outstretched, the cross pattern undeniable.

Kes kneeled and touched the woman's skin. It was cool, but pliant. She checked the wrist for a pulse but couldn't find one.

Kes felt nothing looking at the corpses. She took in the affluent surroundings. The design was minimal, controlled and expensive. There were two photos on the wall. One of a man and a woman in their seventies holding up martinis to the camera. And a black-and-white photograph of the same couple, much younger. Arms around each other's waists, standing proudly before a wooden door with a metal cross above it.

She looked back at the bloodied face and tried to match it to the woman in the photo. She could see the telltale scars of facelifts and the smoothness of Botox on her forehead and around her eyes. Then she saw a small bubble in the woman's bloodied mouth. And another. *Oh, Christ!*

Kes hollered for her team: "She's alive!"

She ran for the kitchen drawers and yanked them open until she found a butcher knife. Harrison was beside her first. She handed him the knife. "Cut the straps." Brownley ran in and stopped short, taking in the spectacle before him.

"Keep Chester out! Get him to call for an ambulance." Brownley pulled himself together and radioed Chester. He was pacing back and forth. Harrison struggled at sawing the leather bands.

"Hurry up," she said.

"I don't want to cut her." His hands were shaking.

Kes scooped her fingers into the woman's mouth and tried to clear her passageway. The blood was warm. The strap across her chin cut free.

"We can slide her down from the blocks," Brownley said. He and Harrison each took a side and reached under the woman's back. "One, two, three," they slid her out.

"Get her on her side," Kes said. Blood poured from the woman's mouth. "Roll her back."

Kes began CPR. She counted chest compressions under her breath.

"I have a protection shield," Harrison said, and retrieved a tightly folded breathing barrier from his police vest. Kes kept counting.

Harrison covered the woman's face and nose with the thin plastic shield and inserted the one-way valve over her mouth. He sat back and tried to steel himself against the blood and gore. "...twenty-five...twenty-six...twenty-seven..." He looked nauseous.

"I'll do it," Kes said. At the thirty count, she leaned over and breathed into the woman's lungs.

They worked in tandem for twenty minutes, waiting for the paramedics to arrive. Their arms were numb. They were drenched in sweat.

The paramedics worked on the woman for another ten minutes. They bagged her and hooked her up to fluids. No pulse. No vitals. They pounded on her chest and shot her with adrenalin. They strapped her to the gurney and on their way out, the lead paramedic looked to Kes and shook his head.

The ambulance siren wailed away and Kes, Harrison, and Brownley stared at each other. Red and wet.

"Fuck," Brownley said. He went to the sink and ran water over his hands. "Fuck, fuck, fuck." He scrubbed and scrubbed. When he turned off the tap, there was only silence.

Kes looked to Harrison, who was standing with his bloodied hands away from his body, his forearms trembling.

She could taste plastic on her lips. She looked to the man still hanging and the outline of blood on the floor where the woman had been posed. She thought of the makeshift crosses in the clearing. The crosses with no names.

"Give me your radio." She took it from Harrison. "Kes for Chester."

"Go for Chester."

"How many died in the school fire?"

"Three. All children."

XXXII.

THE TRUCK SLID FROM THE GRAVEL ROAD ONTO THE HIGHWAY AND Harrison checked it from hitting the shoulder. He shifted gears.

Kes was on the phone with Puck. "Harrison and I are on route to the school. Brownley and Chester are back at the Nichols' house managing the scene...We just missed them, sir. I know they're at the school."

Harrison glanced at her.

"There's a clearing with eight crosses. Three are for the children who died in the fire. The others are for our victims. They're kill markers."

She reached for the grab bar as Harrison took a sharp turn. "If they get there in time, sir, we'll wait for backup."

Harrison could hear Puck's voice get louder.

"Yes, yes. We'll wait for backup." She stared straight ahead. "Our ETA?"

Harrison said, "Five minutes."

"Five minutes. Yes, I heard you, Captain." She hung up.

"What's the plan?" Harrison asked.

"We go in. They're going to run."

"You think killing the Nichols was their end game?"

"I do. They saved them for last." Kes popped a painkiller. Harrison noticed, but didn't say anything.

Their wheels hummed over the bridge and the back end slid on the dirt road. Brush whipped past Kes's window. A low branch scraped the side of the truck.

"Slow down," Kes said. "We need to approach like we're just out for a drive in the woods." She repositioned her holster across her chest and unsnapped the lock strap. Harrison pulled onto the overgrown path leading to the school and slowed to a crawl.

Clouds had blown in from the north and it was getting grey, threatening rain. It was a completely different morning from how it began, as though what they had just witnessed had set a new mood.

"There's a vehicle up ahead." Harrison straightened. They could just make out the gleam of the bumper and a silver-grey hood.

"Stop here. Block the road." Harrison parked across the path and angled the truck to serve as a shield if needed. They quietly got out. Kes indicated to cut through the woods, skirt the clearing. They stepped softly, trying to be quiet. The river's surge helped. They could hear the sound of a mallet on wood.

Approaching the makeshift cemetery, Kes signalled to Harrison to circle around to the other side and she would proceed straight. She kept cover behind the trees until she reached the edge of the clearing. A tall, well-built man was driving a cross into the ground. Another lay ready at his feet. Two being added, facing the school. Seven. They only had five victims. Who were the other two? Other murders? More to come? She scanned the woods across from her looking for Harrison and found him to her left, wedging the suspect between the river and her.

The man paused and stood up. He slowly turned and looked in Kes's direction. She took aim. He didn't see her. He was still and calm. His head tilted up slightly and Kes thought he might be smelling the air.

Harrison's portable radio squawked: "Car 212 en route. ETA twelve minutes."

The man dropped the hammer and bolted for the river. Kes stepped into the clearing. Adrenaline surged, numbing her body.

"Police! Freeze." The man didn't stop. She trained her weapon on his back. "Freeze."

She lowered her aim to his legs, fired, and nicked a tree trunk as he disappeared into the bush.

She and Harrison gave chase. They crashed through the woods, pushing deeper. Her side tweaked, but she barely registered the pain. The brush was thick and tangled. Tree limbs scratched at their arms and thorns snagged their clothes. Kes took cover behind a large spruce and looked to Harrison. "Where can he go?"

"It's woods for miles," he said. "He can't cross the river. The current's too strong with the spring runoff. There's old logging roads east and west..."

"Get Puck to set up the teams there and push in. Let's see if we can flush him out."

Harrison checked his phone. "I don't have a signal." He tried his portable. "Officer 243, requesting backup. Barricade Route 323 east and west. Suspect on foot. Officers approaching from south-southeast along river. Proceed with caution." The radio garbled back, intermittent and incomprehensible.

"Go back to the clearing," Kes said. "Radio them, make sure they got the message."

"I'm not leaving you here."

"I'll stay on this path," she said, pointing out the direction she would take. "Get back as fast as you can. I'm not losing him here. Go!"

Kes took a breath and darted out from behind the tree in the direction the suspect had fled. A light drizzle began to fall, and the fallen pine needles and decay quickly became slippery. Off to her right, the river churned. She slowed. It was quiet. She couldn't hear birds, either.

A movement caught her eye. A branch jostled in the stillness. She ducked under a bower of pine branches and found herself in another small opening, unexpectedly exposed. Her heart was beating fast. She pulled back into the woods and weaved through a tight mesh of young alders. She heard water splashing and pushed her way through the thicket to the riverbank—and there he was, running across the water. It was impossible, the current was too strong. Small white rapids roiled into churning pools edged with a deep brown froth. The man disappeared into the woods across from her.

She ran along the riverbank, looking for a place to ford, and spotted a row of submerged stone-filled cribs connected with planks just below the surface. The first board was only a few inches wide, and spray from the rushing water washed over it. She sensed something near, a charged energy beside her, and swung around, gun drawn.

Harrison appeared from the alder bushes and she lowered her weapon.

"He crossed," she said. Harrison scanned the woods across the river with his weapon. She tucked her gun back in her holster and approached the first plank.

"It's too open," he said. "He could pick you off."

"I don't think he has a weapon."

"You don't know."

He feels too wild. Animal. He doesn't need a gun to kill. "Stay here and co-ordinate the backup."

She steeled her nerves and stepped onto the first board. It bounced underfoot. She gauged the gap of the next span, made a small jump, and landed. Ice-cold water filled her boots. She held her arms out for balance. The last crib was missing its board. She looked to Harrison, his gun trained on the woods. He was shouting directions into his portable, redirecting backup, now in range, to the other side of the river.

Midway, the rapids tumbled with a force that would knock her off. The far bank was only about two metres away, but there was a deep pool in between. She couldn't make it. She looked to the dense camouflage of trees ahead of her. He was going to get away.

Then she saw it in the gurgle of water: boulders just beneath the surface. A submerged natural path, the rocks two to three feet apart. She gauged the rhythm of the gaps. Once she started, she wouldn't be able to stop. She looked to Harrison, who shook his head, then she turned and ran. Not thinking, trusting her feet to find the footings. At the last stone, she hurled herself forward and slammed into the muddy bank. A jolt of pain fired up the stem of her brain, breaking through her body's defenses. She clutched her side and scrabbled back up.

She looked to Harrison, who had started across the river. She swung around and trained her gun on the woods to cover him. Harrison landed beside her.

"I told you to stay back."

He caught his breath. "It's my fault he ran. I have to try to make it right."

They had both screwed up. "This is his home," she said. "This is the place he knows." There was something about the man that didn't add up to the suspect in her head. Something about how he stood. Shoulders down, arms loose. The bow of his head. Something not strong enough, not confident enough...

"I can read a trail," Harrison said. "I've hunted these woods farther back a couple dozen times." He slowly searched the river-bank. "When I was a kid, my father brought me back here. An old trapper owned the land and wouldn't let anyone cut the timber. He believed there was an old gold mine in here somewhere, but no one's ever found it. If it's true, there could be tunnels and possible cave-ins...it's difficult terrain..."

"We're not going back," she said.

"Stay close then." He pointed to a muddy footprint leading over the bank to a narrow deer path. They set out into the damp, misty woods.

An owl hooted from somewhere above them. The brush was thicker on this side, and the trees taller. Soon, they could no longer hear the river. Through the woods, Kes glimpsed a large granite rock. One of the massive boulders dragged south by ancient glaciers over thousands of years. These woods were littered with glacial debris.

Harrison crouched to look at a scuff of freshly overturned dirt and crushed foliage. They moved cautiously, keeping a guard of trees around them. "I think he's barefoot now," Harrison whispered. "The boot prints have stopped."

"Did he step off the trail?"

"I don't know. I've lost him." He retraced the path.

It was colder and gloomier. Kes breathed in the wet scent of earth. *He's here somewhere.* Slowly, she turned, taking in the impasse of trees. *He's close.* She retraced her steps until she could see the boulder again. Two ragged birches pressed against the immense rock, which had a slight tilt to it. One end was burrowed into the earth. Other boulders they had passed were grey and covered in lichen, but this one was bone white. *And the trees.* She hadn't seen birch anywhere back here. They looked almost placed. She softly whistled for Harrison and stepped into the woods.

The boulder was easily twice as tall as her and wider than her motel room. Low to the ground, about waist level, were two impressions. She knelt and ran her fingers over the thin lines seemingly scratched into the stone. They were faded, shallow. She traced the patterns. *Letters?* Two lines: one above, one below. *Names?* Like something a child might do.

Harrison was beside her. She put her finger to her lips. Slowly, they rounded the boulder. There was a narrow opening at the base, where it was held askew by another rock shelf. The tall grass was flattened. She took up position on one side and Harrison the other.

"I don't want to hurt you," she said. "I've been looking for you."

She motioned to Harrison to pull out his phone. *Flashlight,* she mouthed. He turned it on. At her signal, Harrison shone the light into the natural cave.

Kes crouched low, weapon drawn. She took in the stone cavern and sheered granite walls. It reminded her of an ancient Gothic church.

Sitting, with his back to the cold stone, was the man.

He was hugging his knees, eyes to the ground. Rocking slowly back and forth. His feet bare. His worn boots beside him.

"Call in our co-ordinates," she said quietly. "Unarmed suspect."

XXXIII.

IT TOOK TWO UNIFORMS TO EXTRACT THE MAN. IT'S NOT THAT HE fought, but that he refused to move. When they touched him, he curled into a tight ball. It took both officers to pry one arm behind his back. It was as if he had become as heavy and inanimate as the boulder that sheltered him.

The man kept his head bowed on the walk to the car and didn't speak. He was told he had a right to retain counsel, but there wasn't a glimmer of understanding in his eyes. His gaze never shifted from somewhere deep within himself.

Kes watched him the entire time. Only once did he meet her gaze, but then quickly averted his eyes. Ice-blue eyes that she couldn't see inside. His skin was weathered and tanned. Rough whiskers. He could have been handsome. Even beautiful once. The type of man she would have lingered upon in the street or at a bar. But this man had none of the confidence or arrogance that came with his looks, which made him even more attractive.

He was wearing workman's pants and a denim shirt. The cuffs were frayed and blackened. He walked to the squad car barefoot, having ignored the officer's orders to put his boots back on. It was a half-kilometre walk. He didn't betray any indication of pain. His heels were thickly calloused. This was his natural way.

He was slender, but his frame was sinewy. All muscle. His hair was longish and hung in his eyes, but the uneven ends indicated he had cut it himself. His hands, cuffed behind his back, were scarred and hardened. The nails were chewed short. When a bird chirped or fluttered through the trees, his head would cock in its direction.

The terrain was rough and uphill and they were all huffing by the time they reached the police cars. But the man's breathing hadn't changed.

Kes could read nothing from him. He was as still and empty as the rocks underfoot. If he were an animal, she might have passed right by him.

The suspect had been searched, processed, and fingerprinted. Though he didn't have prints. The tips of his fingers had been seared off. The man remained silent throughout and followed the officers quietly down the hall until he saw the small, barred cells. Only then did he resist. It took four officers to shove him in the pen. Once inside, he stood still facing the concrete wall. He stayed there, motionless, for over an hour with his back to the bars.

In the observation room, Kes watched the suspect on the monitor from the single, high camera angle. At hour two, he started to pace back and forth. It reminded her of panthers in a zoo. Captive and seething, trying not to lose their mind.

At hour three, he looked up to the camera. From then on, he sat on the floor with his back to the lens, knees tucked to his chest and arms hugging his legs. The same position in which they had found him. It was like he was willing himself to disappear.

Nearing hour five, Kes went to the conference room. Ten minutes to six and her team was already there. She took a seat on the edge of the table. Puck joined them and leaned against the wall, like it was his job to hold it up. There were dark circles under the men's eyes, and, she imagined, under hers as well.

Brownley still looked shattered from what he had seen earlier. He gripped the edge of the chair like he needed something to hold onto.

She noted the dark bloodstains on his sleeves and bits of evergreen stuck to Harrison's socks. She could see scratches on his shins where his pant leg rose up.

"I'll make this as quick as possible so you can all go home," she said. "It's been a long day. I don't believe the man in custody is the primary killer. He's part of it, but he's not the one calling the shots. At least one killer is still out there."

Harrison cleared his throat. "You said you thought this was his final act. Do you still think so?"

She considered the two extra crosses and the victims they might not have yet found. They felt like endings, not predictors. "I do."

Brownley followed her reasoning. "So, the killer may have fled?"

"I don't think so. We have someone in holding he doesn't want us to have. He doesn't leave loose ends. We need to keep our suspect under constant surveillance. Nobody asleep at the desk." She looked to Puck. "I know we're stretched and I'm happy to take shifts. I'd like you and I to interview him in the morning, Captain."

Puck nodded his agreement.

She looked to the floor. "I know what you all saw today was brutal. I don't know how to tell you to put it away." She recited what they were all taught. "Talk to someone if you need to. Ask your captain for help."

She took in the strained faces of her team, how much this case had put them through. She had so little to offer them as solace, only her own truth. "For me, I've trained myself to look through the horror to see the minutiae. I know that within the carnage is the evidence I need to find the perpetrator. I look from a place that's separate from me." She felt exposed revealing this much to these men she barely knew, but like them, this experience, these deaths, would forever be in their blood. "I just want you to know that I understand if you need to pull back. If you need to step away. It's not weakness to save yourself."

The room was quiet as the men mulled over their decisions. Brownley spoke first. "I'm ready to keep going."

"Me, too," said Chester.

"There's no question," Harrison affirmed.

This was her team. Weary, fractured, but bound together. This was courage.

Brownley straightened and flipped open his notebook, directing everyone back to the case. "We won't get into the lakehouse again until tomorrow. The day was pretty much dedicated to moving the body, documentation, and forensics. Chester and I conducted exterior searches, but there wasn't a clear sign of how the killers gained access to the property. Chester thinks the house was approached from the lake, via boat or canoe...and I agree."

Chester continued. "And the car you found at the school site belonged to the Nichols. I've initiated a country-wide search of unsolved murders that could account for the two additional crosses." He hesitated and then looked up at Kes. "Speaking for myself, I just need to keep working."

The others nodded in agreement.

"So, we keep doing what we're doing."

"And our suspect?" Harrison asked.

"We let him sit for the night. Let the walls close in." A surge of exhaustion washed over her.

Puck stepped forward. "Okay, then I want you all to go home. Take care of yourselves tonight." He looked to Kes. "That means you too, Detective."

XXXV.

KES WALKED INTO THE OCEAN VIEW AND TOOK A SEAT AT THE BAR. The window had been repaired; it was the only one that wasn't coated with a film of salt from the ocean breeze. She looked at the beer taps but couldn't remember what she'd chosen the night she'd been here with her team. The waiter with the braided goatee came around the corner and smiled when he saw her.

"Will you be wanting a pint of your Buccaneer?" He reached up to get a glass from the shelf.

"Yes, I was just trying to remember what it was called."

He poured a pint and placed it in front of her. "Special today is pulled pork on a house-made sourdough roll. Spicy, reminds you that you're alive."

"Perfect."

He left her alone with her drink. She glanced around the restaurant, which was filled with couples enjoying an evening out. She hadn't gone on a date in years. Hadn't had a boyfriend since Henry. She tried to remember how long ago that was—two or three years? Long after her marriage imploded. Even then, he wasn't really a boyfriend. Just someone she slept with for more than a month. She wasn't good at staying. She never felt at home. They'd have sex, and when he fell asleep she'd gather her things and go to her own apartment. The first time, she left a note. After that, it was understood. Their agreement was to keep it light. No commitments. She couldn't really be upset when he found someone else. She had grieved more for herself than for him. She missed having a dinner companion.

The waiter returned to the taps to fill another order. She watched the tilt of the glass and the perfect head. Three glasses, the same amount of foam.

"It's an art," she said, nodding towards the tray of beer.

"Nah," he said. "It's practise. Your body learns the angle and senses the cut-off. My art is painting."

"What do you paint?" She had never understood the conjuring of the imagination. Even as a child, she coloured within the lines and painstakingly tried to keep the palette realistic. Skies were blue and grass was green.

"I'm working on a series of black-and-white landscapes." He pulled out his cellphone and scrolled through until he found a photograph of his work. He passed the phone to Kes. It showed a stunning image of bold cliffs battered by a surging sea. The paint was applied with thick, aggressive strokes and finished with delicate, fine details.

"That's fantastic." And it was. There was a brutality and wildness to it.

"It's one of my bigger pieces. Eight by five feet. It has a power when you stand in front of it. I started with small canvases, but found them confining. It wasn't until I opened the space that I felt free. It completely changed how I paint. Now I have an old sail-maker's loft in town. It's the most beautiful interior, filled with natural light and—"

A bell rang from the kitchen. "Your order's up," he said, heading off to collect her meal. She wondered what it would be like to spend her day chasing beauty. Living inside her own head. Happy.

He returned with her meal and poured her another beer. "You might need this for the spice."

Kes had forgotten how hungry she was. The smell alone made her salivate. She tore into it and didn't stop until her plate was empty. Not when her cheeks flushed red and her eyes watered, and the chili burned her tongue and lips. She relished the pain that verged on delicious joy. The waiter was right. With each bite, she reminded herself that she was alive.

Kes kicked off her shoes and drew back the patio curtains. The town's lights reflecting on the harbour seemed to fracture and reassemble in the water's slight chop, which made her think of hopefulness and how quickly nature rebuilds itself. She slid open the patio door and breathed in the salt air. She laid her jacket and holster over the chair and tucked her gun under her pillow.

She brushed her teeth, and remembering the honey salve, applied it to her wound. After, she dipped her finger in the balm again and brought it to her tongue. It tasted like wildflowers.

She did her stretches. They felt good. Her ribs twinged, but she was healing. Soon she would be running again. She missed the accomplishment of pushing herself beyond her limits. Personal achievement through sheer will and strength. She also missed the dulling of her brain when she reached the pace of the sweet spot, when her mind emptied and it felt like she could run forever. She paused again in front of the patio door and opened it slightly wider before turning off the lights. A cooling salt breeze drifted in.

The freshly made bed smelled of wind and sun and soon she fell asleep.

She was lost at sea on a small raft lashed together by twine that she feared would snap as she rode the heaving waves. In the distance were cliffs, painted in broad strokes of black and white. She tried to paddle towards them, but the wind and current drove her back. There was a pressure on her legs. A dog lying on top of her. Where had the dog come from?

She woke abruptly.

She was on her stomach. One leg over the other. She stayed still, feigning sleep, and kept her breath soft and regular. The room was dark except for the slit in the patio curtains. She listened to the quiet of the night.

"I know you're awake," a man's voice said. "Breathing changes when a person wakes from a deep sleep." The weight on her legs pressed heavier and a hand pushed down lightly on her back. "You were tired. I know that tiredness."

She tried to roll over. She couldn't.

"Don't move, Detective Morris. Relax. It's surprising how little it takes to restrain a person. A simple pressure to counter the physics of human anatomy. One leg over the other."

Kes swallowed the wild panic of being trapped. "Who are you?" She made her voice sound calm and even.

"Oh, you already know that, don't you, Kes?"

"What do you want from me?"

The man took a deep breath. As though he was weary. "I want you to release him. He's not part of this."

"We both want something then," she said. The man smelled of outside. Of earth and trees.

"That's the way of life, isn't it?" he said. "Everyone wanting something."

She tried to turn her head but couldn't. She focused on the darkness. "What should I call you?"

The man laughed. "I know you're better than that, Kes. Call me John, or Mike, whatever you like." He spoke gently. "This has nothing to do with you, and it's finished now."

"Then why are you still here?"

"Because you got in the way. I didn't expect someone like you."

Her legs were numb and her body was beginning to rebel against its confinement. She tried to quell the terror rising in her chest. Her fear of being restrained in a small, dark place. The feeling of being buried alive. She practised what she had been taught. Tried to find a way to anchor herself in the now. She could feel the pillow against her cheek, the smell of laundry detergent. She quieted her mind. If he wanted her dead, she would be by now. She listened intently but couldn't hear him breathe.

"Who is he to you?" She tried to feel the small part of him that still held any vestige of humanness. The place where he held pain and love. "Someone close to you. Someone you trust. Someone you've been with a long time. Someone who will do your bidding. Someone weaker than you."

"You don't know anything," he said.

"I know what happened to you." Her arm was under her chest. Ever so slowly, she slid her hand under the pillow. Her fingertips touched the butt of her gun. "I know about the school. I know what they did to you. I've seen the video."

The man's hand tightened on her calf.

He leaned in and her torso sunk deeper into the mattress. The pressure pinched her knees and her ribs strained. She could feel his breath on her ear. "If you go for that gun, I'll snap your neck before you reach it."

He leaned back. His hand lighter on her spine. "I can feel your heartbeat, Kes," he said. "There you go, slow it down."

She matched her breathing to his. She focused on the heat of his hand and drew it into her. She didn't feel sorrow or rage from him. Or hunger. He was sated. They were simply two animals observing each other.

"I know you don't want to kill me," she said. "I didn't hurt you." She felt only his calm. The calm of someone in control. "You care about him," she said.

She adjusted her profile of the killer. *He has a weakness.* "Let me bring you in. Tell us why you did it, so those bastards' crimes don't die along with them."

"Confess their crimes, while I confess mine?" He considered the offer. "Nobody cared before. Why would it matter now? What I did was just the natural order of things. They got weak and I got strong. The predator became the prey."

His hand was pressing down on the nape of her neck. She was breathing into the pillow. The fabric was too close to her nose.

"They liked to stage things," he said. "I thought it was fitting to do the same for them. But you knew that early, didn't you? What else do you want to know, Detective? Why their particular punishments?"

She breathed through her mouth and the man sat back. His hand remained loosely on her neck. "Should I start with Rakes and Olson?" He paused. "They liked games; they were in charge of recreation and discipline. They kept us in check with demerit points. There were so many ways to get demerit points—talking back, challenging authority, refusing to submit, not keeping quiet, too slow, too fast, crying...

"When you had enough demerits, it was off to the field. A hundred-metre run to a chalk line. There was a ten-second lead and then the other boys would open fire with pellet guns. If they missed or shot wide, they got demerit points. So they didn't miss. Once you crossed the line, there was the fence. You've seen the fence, haven't you?"

Kes lay still. He had come to her. She was meant to listen. He wanted her to know his story. *Another weakness.* He needed her to understand.

"And Doc was in charge of extracurricular activities: selecting, grooming, and educating his "charges"—his word, not mine—as to the proper etiquette. The boys who, shall we say, *protested* were his special projects. He liked to take them on a night walk to the pond, which was really no more than a swamp with a rope strung across. The boys who needed corrections were blindfolded and forced to walk through it using the rope to guide them. It was deep, or maybe it wasn't, up to a boy's chest or neck in parts. Is that deep? If they kept screaming, they had to walk it again and again. There were leeches in the pond. It was quite something to pull them off or have another boy urinate on you to release them. Or you could just wait half an hour until they were full of blood and dropped off on their own."

Kes's eyes had adjusted, and she could make out the grey of the side table and lamp. She listened to the cadence of the man. He sounded educated. A soothing voice that held no emotion.

"Or is it the Gov'nor and Mistress you're most curious about, Kes? The curators. The pimp and matchmaker. The judge and executioner. They did well for themselves, didn't they? Nice house. Nice life." She could hear his smile. "Well, that one was just meant to make them suffer. Slow and painful. The bitch didn't even have drugs in her. I assume you know about the drugs? And I made certain his had worn off by the time the carving began. It seemed fitting to stage versions of their own punishments, don't you think?"

She felt his body tense, a slight shift. A slip in his self-control. She felt her own senses heighten. Now he felt dangerous.

"Or do you want to know how they buggered us? How they mutilated us? Or the things they made us do to them?" He breathed in. "I don't think anyone wants to hear that. Do you, Kes?"

"Yes, I do."

She could feel him smile again. "An idealist. You believe in justice. But nobody came then. And not after. You're too late for justice, Kes. Do you actually think they became fine, upright citizens?"

"I'm sorry nobody stopped them." And she was. "I'm sorry they hurt you."

His nails dug into her leg. She felt the growl in him.

"Don't pity me. I survived. And you..." There was a sadness and disappointment in his voice. "...you tried to protect them. You're not here for them. You're here for me." His voice grew cold and flat. "You knew what they did, but you kept coming."

"It's my job."

"Mine, too." His grip eased, "We're hunters, you and me. It takes patience, doesn't it? Being willing to wait. Allowing what you're tracking to come to you. Striking before they realize you're there."

She tried to shift the power. "He was with you, wasn't he? At the school. And the killings. He's not like you, is he? He's softer." She had bit her cheek and could taste blood and that's when she knew. Knew in the deepest part of herself. *Family.* "He's your brother. Younger. Someone who needed to be protected. You know I'll find out your name and his. There'll be records."

"He's not part of this."

"Then come in and prove his innocence."

"No. A straight exchange. Me for him."

"It doesn't work that way," she said.

"I suppose not. That's a child's wishful thinking. That some-one will do the right thing."

"Five people are dead...or more—"

"They weren't the victims."

Her palm was around the grip of the gun and her finger on the trigger.

His voice was over her right shoulder, two feet back. He lightly squeezed her neck. "You don't want to kill me either, Kes. You invited me in. You wanted to meet me. You left the door open."

He could read her as well as she could read him.

"You're playing a dangerous game, thinking you know me. Unlike you, I am a killer. Let him go."

And with that, the pressure released from her legs. She rolled over, gun raised. But all she saw was the swish of the cur-tain. She jumped from the bed and her legs collapsed beneath her in pins and needles. She dragged herself across the carpet to the glass doors. If she'd seen his fleeing back, she wasn't sure she could have taken the shot, but the night was empty. She pulled herself up and slid the patio door shut, locked it, and drew the curtains tight.

She tore the sheets from the bed and dumped them on the floor, then stripped and got into the shower. She stayed under the too-hot water and scrubbed herself until the small, harsh bar of soap was almost gone and she could no longer feel his hand on her leg.

XXXV.

As she waited for Puck in the observation room Kes's body tingled, electric from the buzz of two pills. One pill too many, she knew. She forced herself to stop rocking, an unconscious soothing to quell the growing sense of claustrophobia crushing in on her in the small space. It wasn't her. It was him she was feeling.

The suspect in the interview room was completely still. Twenty minutes ago, he'd been escorted in and handcuffed to the table. His hands were clasped and he was staring at a spot just beyond the one-way mirror, exactly where she stood. She admired his immense control.

When she arrived at the station, she had tried to walk through without attracting attention, but Susan had greeted her immediately with a bright smile and offers of fresh coffee and blueberry scones, which she'd declined.

She had Brownley escort the suspect while she watched on the security monitor. The man had complied to every command—*Stand up, face the wall, hands behind your back*—passively, as if devoid of will.

The rest of her team was preparing a full search of the last crime scene. Chester was still digging for documentation on the Holy Cross School and thus far had come up empty. It was as if it had been scoured from existence. She had five murders and seven kill markers and not a shred of physical evidence linking the crimes to the man in custody, or the one who had visited her last night.

She hadn't told her team about that. What would she tell them? That she had used herself as bait? That she hadn't taken the shot? That the killer had confessed to her? Someone whom she couldn't identify, but whose scent she could still smell. He would come to them. She had what he wanted.

Puck entered and Kes noted the coffee stain on his tie. He stood alongside her and looked to the man. "The night guard said he didn't move or make 'a sound all night." He sounded tired. "He doesn't look much like a killer."

"I once arrested the sweetest woman," Kes said. "Petite, pretty, a wonderful smile. She poisoned eight people. She never stopped smiling as she recounted every detail of watching them die."

Puck checked his watch. "You have five hours before we have to charge him or release him. We need evidence." He looked to her. "Are you sure about this, Kes?"

"I am." She couldn't tell him how she knew. Not yet. Not until she had to. He'd shut them down. "I know he didn't do it alone, sir. He's too submissive. He's not the architect. But he's part of it. If he's released, we'll never find him again."

"When twenty-four hours are up, we cut him loose. You know the law."

"Captain, I'd like to go in alone. I don't think he'll respond well to men."

"I'll be watching from here." She headed for the door. "And Detective Morris, the interview will be recorded."

She held up her phone in acknowledgment.

Kes set a stack of photos face-down and slid a paper cup across the table, stopping a few inches from the man's chained hands. His stare shifted to a spot on the table.

"You must be thirsty." He didn't budge. The wooden chair was short and the man was tall, which forced him into an uncomfortable-looking curled position with his knees high. She placed her phone between them and hit record.

"I'm Detective Morris; this interview is being recorded." She checked that the sound levels were running. "You've been informed that you have the right to retain and instruct counsel. By your silence, you are agreeing to waive this right."

She waited ten seconds. "The subject has remained silent. I'm going to ask you a few questions. I'm hoping you can help us. You were picked up at the former site of the Holy Cross School for Boys. A vehicle registered to Harold Nicholson, a.k.a. Nichols, was also found on site. He and his wife, Martha, were murdered the same day. You were in the process of erecting two wooden crosses."

The stillness of the man felt empty and detached. His ice-blue eyes were vacant.

"I think you were erecting the crosses for the murder victims. I think the additional crosses were for other victims. But there wasn't any blood on you. I don't think you were the one who did the killings."

She could read nothing from him. She flipped over a photograph of the school and pushed it across the table.

"Did you go to this school?" She touched the photograph, keeping her hand close to his. "I know what happened there." His breathing didn't change. "I saw a video of what was done to the boys there." She watched his face for a flush of blood. She looked to his carotid for a racing pulse. Nothing.

She turned over the morgue photos of the victims and laid them one by one alongside the school photo. "I know that these were the perpetrators. I know they were all involved with the school." She placed her hand on the last two images. "I know that these two, the Gov'nor and the Mistress, were in charge."

The man didn't respond. Didn't shift his gaze. She leaned in closer, keeping just out of reach of his chained hands.

"I understand wanting to kill them." She could feel Puck's caution behind the glass, *Careful where you go.* "I understand wanting to make them suffer for what they did. After all these years of them getting away with it, they finally paid. I would have wanted them dead. I would have wanted to kill them." She trailed her fingers over the photos, then gathered them up and flipped them over. She picked up the two Polaroids and stared at them. "You were so young then."

She turned over the photo of the boys' soccer team. "Are you one of these boys?"

The man betrayed nothing. She laid down the other photo of the young boy posing for the camera. She saw a small twitch at the corner of his eye. Fleeting, then gone. "Do you know this boy?"

She let the image stay between them. The man's eyes had shifted focus. He was looking at the photograph.

"He seems happy." She picked up the image and the man's gaze shifted back to a vacant space between them. "But photos can lie, can't they?" She picked up the other Polaroid. "This one looks like a thousand other team shots. No one can see their pain. No one ever saw it, did they? You wanted to make certain everyone saw it this time."

The man had disappeared inside himself again. She had lost him, before she had even reached him. She set the photos down over the phone, muffling the mic with her hand. She leaned forward and stared at the same empty space between them, lowering her head away from the security camera.

"Your brother came to me last night," she said quietly.

The man's piercing eyes looked up and she held his stare.

"He wants me to let you go. He said you had nothing to do with it. Convince me. Talk to me." She pushed harder. "I *will* get him."

Puck rapped on the one-way mirror and Kes sat back, uncovering the phone, and inadvertently knocked over the cup of water. In a flash, the man's hand shot forward the length of the chain and caught it before it tipped. He sat the cup upright, close to Kes and beyond the safety line demarcated on the table.

The door slammed open and Puck charged in. "Hands back!"

Kes stopped him. "It's okay." She looked to the man, but he had returned to his former position, hands clasped, eyes fixed inward. But she had seen the flash of his unfettered wildness.

XXXVI.

WHEN KES ENTERED THE CONFERENCE ROOM, HER TEAM FELL QUIET. She sat on the edge of the table and took a moment to look at each of the men.

Brownley was wearing the same shirt as the night before, and his brown shoes with their scuffed toes were still marred with mud from the day she'd first met him at the rifle range. She had found him to be loyal, diligent, and quietly perseverant. Old school. When he went home at night, she imagined he took off his shoes and tie, cracked a beer, and gave himself completely to the quiet life he loved with Susan.

Chester had the squirrelly energy of a mind that was always multi-tasking. He saw everything as a problem to logically solve. He spent more time, on and off the job, with computers than humans. He was someone who liked the precision of thinking and action. She looked at his hands. These were not detective hands. They were hardened from woodworking and fishing. A man who stilled his mind with physical labour.

And Harrison. His eyes were tired. And they held such loss. Loss of a marriage, of a child away, and an empty home. He had a small paunch and had probably started drinking more at night. He had seen too much, too soon, on this case, but he held it tight. Even when afraid, he would step forward. He was a man who tried to live by a personal creed of integrity. A good man.

She could sense these deepest parts of them. She hadn't lost her ability to read people. It was just him, the man in the cell, who eluded her.

Puck stepped in and went to his usual spot beside the door and leaned against the wall. He had taken up that perch so many times, the paint had slightly darkened.

"He's not talking," she said. "We only have a few hours before we have to cut him loose."

"What the hell?" Harrison exploded. "We found him with the victim's car!"

"There's no forensic evidence connecting him. No blood, no prints, no DNA. No confession. We don't have enough to charge him."

"But we know he's guilty!" He looked to the others to back him up.

"Cool down," Brownley cautioned.

Harrison looked to Kes in disbelief. "So that's it? All this death and fucking horror? My kid shoots a man because of him and he walks?"

Kes stood up. "I didn't say it's over. I said we have more to do. Get Sally and Doug to pick up Billy Cochrane. Let's see if he can ID our guy. Brownley, take an officer and finish up at the Nichols' house." She needed them to come together.

"The man we have is not our primary suspect. He didn't operate alone. Chester, I need you to get into the juvenile and foster-care files again, five to ten years prior to the school fire. Harrison will assist." She didn't want him in the field until he got himself in check. "Look for brothers in the system. The captain will help you put on the pressure. There's someone else out there. These two have been together their entire lives. They've lived through unimaginable hell and never left each other. One is the protector. He won't leave that man in there behind."

Puck eyed her narrowly. "What are you saying, Kes?"

"Charge him. I need more time. We'll get the evidence. And I want an additional team on tonight. Full security. He's going to come in."

"Why would you think that?" Puck asked sternly.

She held his stare. "Because he told me, sir. Him in exchange for his brother."

"In my office now, Detective!" Puck slammed the door on his way out.

Kes turned to her team. "Find me something."

The thin walls and doors did little to muffle Puck's voice as he berated Kes.

Susan eventually got up and shut the door between the front desk and the offices. Kes took the dressing-down and focused on a spot over Puck's head, letting words like *dangerous, protocols*, and *commanding officer* spill around her. When he had finished venting his displeasure, she finally spoke.

"Respectfully, sir, we only have hours left. This isn't helping us find what we need to keep our suspect locked up. I need you to contact the media and set up a story that we have a suspect in custody, who will be charged, and will be transferred to federal custody tomorrow. We need his brother to think we have more than we do."

"You want me to lie."

"Mislead. Stall. Buy us time. He will come, sir. And when he does, I want to have enough to convict them."

Puck couldn't hide his exasperation in his voice. "You are dangerously riding the line, Detective Morris, and my patience."

"He came to me, sir. He'll come to me again."

Puck's voice rose. "You think he's going to turn himself in? A man capable of such atrocities? *This* is who you're going to trust?"

She responded with calm, her head deferred in respect. "I think he would do anything to save his brother. Even sacrifice himself. I think, sir—*I know*—that he's done it his entire life."

She looked directly at Puck. He looked older these last few days. Deep worry etched his face. The lightness of the man who enjoyed golf after work and had earned his community's respect with his gentle, fair approach had dimmed. There was a vial of antacids on his desk and the normally neatly organized files were piled haphazardly. One folder was ringed with a coffee stain. Even his clothes had lost their crispness.

"He's coming, sir. Whether we're prepared or not."

Puck pondered the implications. "Two officers, two detectives, and a detail outside."

"One officer. Myself. One detective. And a detail outside. I need him to feel safe."

Puck evaluated the risks and the detective standing before him. "I want to know every beat as it happens. Do you understand?"

"Yes, sir."

"This is my family, Kes. This isn't just a job for me. All protocols will be followed to keep my family safe."

"That's what I'm trying to do, sir."

Puck checked his watch and sighed. "Then stop wasting time."

XXXVII.

Billy Cochrane was roused from sleep by Sally and Doug. It took some convincing to assure him he was just coming in to give an ID. It was only when Doug started poking around a pile of suspicious marine parts from various boats that Billy decided he would do whatever he could to help. But he kept reiterating that he "Didn't know nothing." Claimed he'd told the woman detective, "the pretty one with the eyes that look through you," everything already.

Kes greeted Billy warmly and thanked him for coming back in. She led him down the hall and kept up small talk about the fine spring weather to lull him into a friendly comfort. When she rounded the corner to the holding cells, she went quiet.

Billy kept rambling on about nothing and almost bumped into Kes when she stopped short and stepped aside. Billy shut up then. He stared at the man in the cell who was crouched in the back corner.

"Do you know this man?" Kes watched Billy's face.

He shook his head. "No."

"Never seen him before?"

Billy's eyes shifted to the floor, to the wall.

"Look at him again."

Billy settled on the man again. "No, ma'am."

"That's not who paid you to follow me?"

"No, definitely not." He said it with conviction. He was telling the truth.

Kes stepped closer to the bars. "Look up," she said to the suspect. The man's head slowly lifted.

"Step closer," she said to Billy. He did, and steadied himself with one hand on the cell bar. An unconscious grip. *For strength or courage?* The man stared emptily at Billy, then lowered his head again. Not a flicker of recognition.

Kes looked at Billy, who smiled weakly. "Is that it?" His ears had flushed red. When he lowered his arm in relief, she glimpsed his scarred wrist.

"No," she said. "I have a few more questions."

She escorted him to the small interview room and as she passed Harrison, she said, "Come with me." She directed Billy to take a seat in the corner. The table was tight to his belly. Kes sat across from him. Harrison stayed at the door.

"I really appreciate you coming in," she said. "It was a slim chance, but we hoped we might get lucky."

"Happy to help, that's for sure." Billy's hands were fidgeting, his thumb absently rubbing his wrist just below the cuff of his shirt.

"I couldn't help but notice the scar on your wrist, Billy. That looks like a burn."

He tugged his sleeve down. "Yeah, a long time ago."

Kes stared at him hard. She looked to Harrison. "Would you get the photos for me, please?"

Harrison stepped out and Kes kept her gaze fixed on Billy. "How old are you?"

"Thirty-two."

"I think you told me before that you had always lived around here?"

"Yep." He shuffled in his chair. *Lie*, she thought.

Harrison returned with the photos. Kes set them on the table face-down and retrieved her phone. "I'm going to record this, Billy. Sometimes my memory can't hold it all. Is that okay with you?" She laid the phone between them.

"I can't see why he'd mind," Harrison pressured.

"Yeah, no, that's fine."

Kes ID'd the recording: "Interview with Billy Cochrane with

Detective Kes Morris, lead, and Officer Cooper Harrison present." She slid the phone closer to Billy.

"Billy, have you ever heard of the Holy Cross School for Boys?" Her eyes sharpened.

"No," he said. He swallowed. *Lie.*

"You would have been young. You might not remember it. It burned down. How old did you say you were again?"

"Thirty-two."

"That would have made you about nine years old then. But you've never heard of it?"

"No."

"Where did you go to school, Billy?"

"Up South Bay way, a little community school, but I never finished. It's not around no more. Got tore down."

"I was wondering because of the scar on your arm. Do you mind rolling up your sleeve?"

"I don't see what that's gotta do with anything."

"Well, the man in custody, I think he went to the Holy Cross School for Boys. I think he was there when it burned down. So, I'd like to see your arm and I'd like you to tell me how you got that burn."

Billy's carotid was pumping.

"Roll up your sleeve, Billy."

Billy's eyes darted between Kes and Harrison. "Don't you need a warrant for that?"

"We could, but that would make me suspect you're hiding something, rather than trying to help us."

Billy reluctantly rolled up his sleeve. His forearm was a thick braid of scar tissue. "I got it playing around a wood stove when I was kid. Fell onto it."

The scars flared around his arm. They didn't have the sharp, hard edge of the branding of metal on skin.

"We know what happened at that school, Billy. What happened to the boys." Kes spoke gently. Billy rolled his sleeve back down and tugged it to make sure the scars were covered. He was working hard to hide himself. "But you don't remember that place?"

"No," he said.

"Billy, I don't believe a stranger came up to you and offered you a pile of money to watch me." Her fingers fanned the corners of the photographs.

"It's what happened." He couldn't meet her eyes.

"The man in the cell is suspected of torturing and killing five people, likely more."

"I don't know him." She could feel the bounce of his leg under the table.

"The people he killed ran the school, but I don't think he did it by himself."

"Well, it sure as hell wasn't me."

"But taking money from a murderer, interfering with an investigation...that could make you an accomplice, an accessory after the fact. That's a long, life sentence in the penitentiary." She watched for her way in. "I know the man in the cell has a brother."

Billy's fidgeting stilled. She flipped over the photos of the victims.

"Jesus Christ." Billy looked away. "I didn't have nothing to do with that!" He shielded his eyes with his hands, not wanting to see. She could see scars on his other wrist.

"It's okay, Billy. You don't have to look. I'll tell you their names, and maybe you'll recall something: Rakes, Olson, Doc Wilson, these two went by Gov'nor and Mistress. Ever heard of them?"

"No," he said adamantly.

"The killers wanted them to hurt. It was slow and painful. Punishing." She turned the photos back over. "I've put the photos away, Billy." He looked up.

"When I check the school's records am I going to find your name there, Billy?" She selected another photo and slid it towards him. The one of the boys posed in their soccer uniforms.

"I was always curious about this boy." She pointed to one of the children. "He's younger than the others. Too small to play soccer with them. But there he is. And you see those boys behind him? They each have a hand on his shoulder. He had friends. Is that little boy you, Billy?"

"No," he said. But his eyes said otherwise.

"I'm going to arrest someone, Billy. I have one person in custody and I need to get the other. I'm under pressure to deliver, you know how it is. Whether it's you or him, I don't really care. Guilty is guilty. Case closed. And I don't buy your story, Billy."

Kes pushed back her chair. "Charge him as an accomplice to murder. I know enough."

"You don't know shit," Billy said. "I didn't kill no one! And the one you got, he didn't do nothing neither. You're setting him up. He's not like that."

"What's his name?"

"That guy in there never came to me."

"His name?"

Billy growled, "Mason."

"Was it his brother then who came to you? Hired you to keep an eye on me?"

Billy sat back, surprised she knew about a brother.

"I've talked to him," she said. "I know what he's capable of. I know he doesn't leave loose ends. Are you a loose end, Billy?"

"I hadn't seen him in over twenty years. He came back and looked me up. He knew I could use the money." He clasped his hands on the table. Separating himself from her. "We didn't talk nothing about the old days, just how we were now. He looked good. I figured you were an old girlfriend and he wanted to know who you were hanging with. That's all." His thumb lightly traced the scar on his wrist.

"His name, Billy." She could smell his fear. Metallic and bitter. "Your friends are murderers."

"No." His grip tightened.

"Sadists."

"No." She could see the strain of his muscles holding himself in.

"By protecting them, you're going to serve time. Why would you protect these animals?"

He slammed the table. "You don't know nothing about them!" His eyes blazed, betraying the fire in him. Harrison stepped forward, but Kes stayed him with her hand.

"How did you get burned, Billy?" she pushed, knowing he wanted to set them straight. He wanted them to know the truth. "Help me understand."

His jawline tightened and his eyes hardened. "I was seven when I was sent to that hellhole. I had nobody. But they saw me and they protected me. They got me out of there and took care of me. They saved me. So you're *never* gonna convince me that what they did was wrong."

"How did you get burned, Billy?"

His hand went to his arm. "They were going to make it stop and I wanted to help. They said I was too young. But I had matches too." He looked past Kes and his gaze shifted upward, like he was a small child seeing that night again.

"The curtains went right up. They already had the main buildings burning. Kids were running, everybody was supposed to get out. But the curtains lit up and flames was climbing the walls and ceiling and around the door. I tried to pull them down, but then the fire was on me." He looked to his scarred arms. "My sleeves were on fire. They came back for us. For me. He come through the door, Mason right behind him, always behind him, and dragged us kids out. They almost got us all. They got me."

He looked back to her, his eyes clouded with sorrow. "They thought if the school was gone, we'd be safe. They didn't kill those boys. I did that."

He pointed to the morgue photos. "Every one of those bastards deserved to die. I wish I had the courage to have done it. If they did it, then they're fuckin' heroes."

"What's his name, Billy?"

He leaned defiantly back in his chair. "Caleb. Caleb Andrews. Best friend I ever had. He was like a brother. I wouldn't be here if it weren't for him. He's better than anyone in this room. Better than all of you."

She looked at the photo of the small boy and two older boys right behind him. "Mason," she said, pointing to one. And the other, "Caleb." By Billy's silence, she knew she had guessed correctly.

Kes ended the interview and turned off the recorder. The overhead lights hummed in the quiet. She gathered up the photos and headed for the door. "Let him go." She looked back at Billy. "Don't leave the area."

As she stepped into the corridor, Puck exited the observation room. "You have whatever you need," he said.

XXXIII.

THE SUN WAS LOW AND THE TEAM HAD BEEN GRAVITATING TO THE conference room throughout the afternoon. Laptops and additional chairs had been pulled in as they set up makeshift desks.

Kes was perusing the medical examiner's reports and the latest crime scene photos. Puck had leaked a story to the media that a suspect was in custody and would soon be transferred. Harrison was updating the photos and maps. At the top of the board was an empty space for *Caleb Andrews* and beside him a mugshot of *Mason Andrews*, head slightly bowed and eyes focused beneath the lens.

A hit had been found on the brothers through Child Protection services records. Caleb and Mason Andrews had been placed in foster care at the ages of six and four. Their file included reports of multiple transfers, runaway attempts, and numerous infractions for fighting and disruption. There were various caseworkers' notes about the immense bond of the brothers and that separation was not recommended. The trail went cold with the brothers' relocation to a federal program for troubled boys at the ages of twelve and ten. All records of that time were missing.

After the school burned down, the brothers seemed to go completely off the grid for twenty-five years. It was a fluke that Harrison had widened the search to include all government records and had gotten a recent hit on a local property transfer in their names. One hundred and twelve acres. Adjacent to the former school grounds.

The previous owner was Barkley Smith, a trapper who'd lived in the backwoods. He'd died the previous year at the age of ninety-seven. No living relatives. He'd deeded the land to the brothers. Their connection was unknown.

Brownley returned from the Gov'nor's residence with half a dozen boxes filled with videotapes. The stash had been found locked in a safe hidden at the back of a closet. Chester regaled the team with the story of how he had found it. He had passed over it twice, but kept going back. He just had a sense that something was off. As it turned out, there was a false back that had shaved three inches off the closet. He had trusted his gut.

Brownley and Chester were painstakingly labelling the tapes into evidence. Nobody could bring themselves to look at them yet.

The team worked in sync, sharing information, passing paperwork across the table, and offering suggestions when one trail went cold to open another. They had an unconscious need to be close together.

Susan brought in coffee and sandwiches on baked bread with real shaved ham and lots of vegetables, which they all dug into with gratitude. The last hour had grown quiet with the realization that the small steps forward only linked the past crimes of the deceased; they did nothing to tie the suspects to the present-day murders.

At six, Puck took his regular spot by the door and Kes moved to the front of the room. "Captain Puck has given a statement to the media, which should be on the news now, inferring that we will be transferring our suspect in the morning. At this point, we do not have any physical evidence connecting the killers to the scenes."

She glanced to the board, where every connecting line led back to the brothers. "But we know they did it. The killers have controlled this narrative. Giving us only what they want us to find. It has been carefully calculated and meticulously orchestrated. They designed the game and the rules."

She stood tall and felt the low rub of pain. "He'll come tonight. We have what he wants. For the first time, he's not in control. He has to come to us. We know what these men are capable of, but thus far their focus has been on those who hurt them. Tonight, there will be an additional detail watching the station. I've requested minimal personnel—the desk sergeant, myself, and one other detective to keep watch with me."

Each member of her team raised a hand, volunteering to join her. She smiled. It was the first time she could remember doing so on this case. "I would take all of you, anytime, every time...but tonight, I'm asking Brownley."

"Absolutely," he said.

"I'll come in," Harrison stated. "Off the clock."

"Me, too." Chester said.

"I'm sorry." She understood they wanted to see it through to the end. "But I don't want to escalate or trigger the suspect to fight back. We need to keep our numbers small. We're not cornering him. We're letting him come in. It has to be this way."

The men thought about it. They weren't satisfied, but they knew her decision was made.

Kes looked to Puck, whose eyes were fixed on her. She could almost hear him thinking *Don't be wrong.*

Cots had been brought into the conference room and Brownley was taking a nap. It was 22:20 and all was quiet. Kes had promised to wake him in two hours, unless something transpired sooner.

It was odd being in the quiet and emptiness of the station after-hours, and she found herself wandering up and down the halls, walking the perimeter to keep herself alert. She filled her coffee cup again. She had taken one of her pills an hour ago and it had just kicked in. No painkillers tonight. She needed that sharp edge. She was acutely aware of every sound and movement. At the front desk, Spence turned a page of his newspaper and she could hear it rub against his fingertips.

She passed by the front door again and glanced to the unmarked car parked down the street. The night was still, the town already asleep or dozing off to the television. Few houses had lights on inside. The streets were empty. There wasn't even a stray cat or dog to distract her.

Puck was calling every hour on the hour for a status report. Spence would look to Kes and reply, "Nothing to report." She didn't think he would make it to the 23:00 check. He was accustomed to going to bed early. She had assured him they would call if the status changed.

This was the pace of a small-town police department. Night shift might respond to infrequent noise complaints, usually involving out-of-town partiers or young kids burning rubber on the back roads. More likely, the calls would be medical emergencies. The majority of the population in the area were retirees, who could afford to live in this picturesque but expensive town. But mostly, the night brought highway accidents.

Spence turned another page. Beside him was a monitor with multiple camera angles: one outside the front door covering the entrance, another angled up the street for a wide view, one behind the precinct on the impound lot, and one each inside the interview room and holding cell.

She stepped in closer to look at Mason curled into the fetal position on the bench, his face to the cement wall. He hadn't moved in hours. On the other bench was his untouched supper.

Spence had adapted to Kes's pacing and no longer responded to her walking up to his desk. He had been doing night shift for three years and wasn't accustomed to having anyone else in his space, but he seemed relieved she didn't expect him to fill the night with chit-chat.

Puck had told her Spence wasn't a big talker, but an exceptional co-coordinator under pressure. The radio chattered and squawked with checks, 10-100 breaks, and officers who just wanted to hear another voice as they sat in their cars. Mostly there was silence, which meant it was a good night.

Kes headed back down the hall past the cramped offices. For the last hour she had been playing a game with herself, memorizing what was on each desk. She hadn't missed an item yet from her initial walk-by. She could recall Susan's chipped coffee mug with a red heart, two small stuffed bears hugging each other, two purple pens, and single box of paperclips.

Chester's desk was more chaotic—stacked with files, a splay of computer cables, multiple coffee cups on the go, two of which were unwashed, and a framed photograph of a large dog with a kerchief around its neck. She didn't remember Chester mentioning he had a dog. Nor were his clothes covered in dog hair. She assumed it was deceased.

Brownley's desk was surprisingly neat. She expected it to be more relaxed, but his desktop was completely clear. The day's work filed away. There was one clean coffee mug at the edge of the table, two pouches of sugar, a blank notepad, and a pen by the phone. He was set for the next day.

She paused by the conference room and could hear Brownley snoring. *Good*, she thought, *let him sleep*. She headed to the cell. The overhead light was on and the sound, dampened by the cement blocks, had a deeper quiet back here.

She watched the man breathe. She could tell he wasn't sleeping. Quietly she said, "Mason."

He didn't betray that he had heard her.

"I know your brother's name." His foot moved ever so slightly. The soles of his boots were worn thin. The shoelaces had been removed, along with his belt, as a precaution. "Caleb."

He seemed to become even stiller. His breath had slowed.

"He told me what he did and why. I know what they did to you, Mason."

She didn't expect him to answer. He hadn't offered anything yet. It had been almost forty hours of silence.

"I spoke to Billy Cochrane, too. He told me about the fire. He told me how you and Caleb saved him. I know you didn't want any of those boys to die."

She watched his back, the small rise and fall of his breath. She imagined his eyes were open, staring at the wall. She tried to lure him to her.

"Your brother wants to see you," she said.

Mason looked over his shoulder. He looked tired, but his icy eyes had lost none of their coldness, like she was being probed for the truth.

"I can make that happen," she said. "If you tell me what you know."

She saw him swallow and for a moment, she thought he might just speak. He glanced up to the security camera and turned back to the wall.

She watched him for another ten minutes. She practised being as still as him. Her calves grew tight, her lower back pinched, and her ribs dully ached. She let her mind quiet and her body disappear. She tried to sense who he was, but all she could feel was a dark void pulling her in. Her arms chilled and deep inside, a voice called her back. *Don't follow him in.* She looked to Mason, as motionless as a corpse, and stepped away.

XXXIX.

Kᴇꜱ'ꜱ ᴇʏᴇꜱ ᴡᴇʀᴇ ɪᴛᴄʜʏ ᴀɴᴅ ᴅʀʏ. Sʜᴇ ᴡᴀꜱ ʟʏɪɴɢ ᴏɴ ᴀ ᴄᴏᴛ, ᴛʀʏɪɴɢ ᴛᴏ rest her racing mind. Brownley had awoken an hour ago and chastised her for not waking him sooner.

She could smell coffee brewing. The lights were off, but she could decipher the outlines of the photos and markings on the whiteboard. She didn't need to see it; she could visualize every detail. She closed her eyes and sifted through the pieces, looking for the hard evidence that continued to elude her.

Just before midnight, there was an MVA involving a deer on the highway not far out of town, but nothing since. As expected, Puck had stopped calling. She checked her watch: 01:20. She closed her eyes and didn't think she had fallen asleep, but when she was woken by a rap on the door it was 02:45.

Brownley stuck his head in. "Think you should hear this—"
She was on her way before he finished the sentence. Her head swam as she tried to focus back into consciousness.

He updated her as they walked. "Call came in twenty minutes ago, a fire out Osprey Lake way. First on scene confirmed it's the Nichols' place. It's completely engulfed. Crews are trying to keep it from spreading to the woods."

"Who called it in?"

"Anonymous. Hung up."

Spence was leaning in close to the radio, listening to the fire department's communications. He looked up to Kes and then back to his monitors.

"Three trucks are responding," he said. "One volunteer department. There's only one road in. But there's no wind

206

tonight and it's been damp. No other structures are threatened yet, but we have a car en route to check other homes in the area and initiate evacuation if conditions change."

Kes went to the window and looked up and down the street. Still empty.

"Check on the surveillance team."

Spence called in: "583 to 243, check."

"Good check" came back.

She returned to the monitor and scrutinized the various angles. Nothing outside. In the cell, Mason was still in the same position.

Brownley asked, "What are you thinking?"

A dispatch alert sounded with a detachment code. "There's another fire," Spence said. "This one in town."

"What's the address?" Kes asked.

"Hobson Road."

Brownley looked to Kes, "Doc's house."

The station phone rang and Spence picked up. "Police. Yes...yes...we're aware of the situation. Emergency crews are en route." He typed into his computer, pulling up a stream of communications. "Stand by, please." He put on his earpiece. "This is 583. South Bay and East Shore fire departments are standing by, need to direct to 343 Hobson Road."

The radio squawked. "Car 223: we have a house fire. Adjacent homes under threat, requesting assistance to evacuate the surrounding property."

Spence muttered to himself, "We don't have anyone." He rubbed his forehead while the radios chattered.

"You have our detail," Kes said.

"Not an option."

"Call Puck." She didn't have time to argue.

Spence placed the call as he continued managing logistics.

She looked to Brownley. "Suit up." He headed to retrieve their vests.

"Stand by, sir," Spence calmly directed through his headset and switched to radio coms. "Two trucks en route to Hobson

Road, ETA 2 minutes." The lines continued to light up. He turned his attention back to the phone. "Sorry to wake you, Captain—"

"Is that him?" Kes waved to Spence to hand over the receiver. "Captain, we have two fires—at Doc's and the Gov'nor's. They need additional police to evacuate and cordon off Hobson Road. I'm releasing our detail. Spence needs authorization."

Brownley returned with her vest. She motioned to Spence to put on his, too.

"Sir, he's coming in. He wants the police pulled back...Yes, I'm sure...we don't need them here." She listened as she tightened her vest. "Yes, sir."

Kes passed the phone back to Spence. "Cut them loose." In the distance she could hear sirens.

Spence redirected the detail. The surveillance car's lights came on and sped away.

She looked to Spence and Brownley. "When he comes in, full alert. Keep a minimum six-foot radius. Weapons at ready. Once we let him in, Spence, you pat him down and then stay on the periphery. Your job is to keep reporting to Puck and monitoring the teams out there. I don't want any heroes tonight. Understood?"

"Business as usual." Spence turned back to the monitors and picked up mid-conversation, completely aware of every call that had been transpiring in the background.

She looked to Brownley. "Hang back and give him space, okay? Follow my lead."

Kes looked to the monitors. Mason was standing in the middle of the cell facing the door, like he was expecting company.

She positioned herself directly in front of the entrance.

Brownley stayed behind her and off to the side, where he had the broadest vantage point to cover her.

The radios continued to squawk updates. Both buildings were fully engulfed. Water was being pulled from the lake for the Osprey fire. House-to-house checks were underway on Hobson Road.

Kes could envision the scene. People would be staggering into the street in their bedclothes now. Police would be trying to convince them to leave everything behind, while they ran around grabbing computers and phones, children and pets.

She knew he would have set the fires so they could be contained. Either through luck or skill, she doubted there would be damage to any other property. He would have timed how long it would take emergency crews to arrive and get it under control. He was probably the anonymous caller.

A man was approaching the station. His head was down. Sandy-brown hair. Tall. Thin. Dark shirt, jeans. Workboots. He could be anyone coming off the docks.

XL.

"CALL PUCK," KES SAID CALMLY, "LET HIM KNOW HE'S HERE." SPENCE immediately dialled. The switchboard continued to flash and the radio crackled with fire and police communications.

The man walked straight to the locked glass doors. He moved with a confidence and ease that made him appear approachable, and yet not someone to screw with. He had the same gait as Mason, someone who felt the ground beneath him.

He stopped at the entrance. He was older, his face more weathered, but he had the same lithe, muscular body as his brother. The same blue eyes, but harder in their intensity. The same tight jaw that couldn't be read. He and Kes stared at each other with equal calm. Breath for breath. Neither looked away. She felt the crawl of something around her heart. Something fierce and untamed. This was the man who had been in her room.

"Tell him to put his hands up," Kes said to Spence, who reached for the intercom. Before he could speak, the man outside the doors raised his arms above his head. He had read her lips.

She turned to Brownley, his weapon at ready. "Don't let your guard down."

"You neither," he said.

"Spence, don't approach until I say so."

She looked back to the man. In the top corner of the glass door, a spider was making a web. It appeared to be hanging in limbo. The man followed her gaze to the spider and then back to her. So relaxed.

"Buzz him in," she said. "Tell him one hand only to open it, keep the other in the air." She was six feet from the threshold. She unclasped her holster and kept a hand on her weapon. Spence repeated her instructions over the intercom and pressed the lock release.

Caleb pushed open the door.

"Step in, both hands above your head," she said.

The door shut behind him and re-locked.

"Hello, Kes."

"We need to search you," she said.

"Of course." He responded as though they were old friends. His non-threatening posture and loose calm were disarming.

"If you move, you will be shot," she said.

"Understood."

She thought she detected bemusement in his eyes. The hint of a smile. "Hands on the back of your head. Search him."

Caleb kept his focus on Kes as Spence hobbled around the desk. His foot scuffed the floor. "I see you brought your finest, Kes."

Spence frisked him from behind, starting at his elbows, then patted down his biceps, across his shoulders, down his back, under his arms, across his chest, belly, pockets back and front, crotch, and down both legs. Spence stepped back six feet.

"Clean," he said.

Kes held Caleb's gaze, which hadn't faltered. She could hear Brownley's even breath behind her. The phone lines were ringing.

"You can go back to your desk," she said. Spence hesitated, but complied. He kept his eye on the suspect even as he answered the calls.

"It's a beautiful night," Caleb said. "It's begun to warm up. Have you noticed the birds are back?"

"There's a couple of fires in town tonight," she said. "Would you know anything about that?"

"I suppose those old wooden structures are at risk for that. Hope nobody gets hurt. May I?" He indicated lowering his arms.

"Slowly, hands at your side."

He complied, palms outward to show his deference. His hands were scarred and hardened. "Is my brother safe?"

Kes heard a hesitation in his question, as though *safe* hadn't been quite the right word. "Yes," she said.

"I want to see him. Make sure he's still here. There's a lot of rumours going around town." He looked to Brownley, as though gauging his adversary and dismissing him. Brownley held his stare.

"I have a few questions for you first," Kes said, drawing him back to her.

"Any way I can help," Caleb said.

"Shall I cuff him?" Brownley asked.

"Ah, he speaks." But he didn't take his eyes off Kes. "I've come voluntarily to offer information. I don't believe you have any evidence to warrant an arrest or handcuffs. Not yet anyway. I believe if I had counsel that's what they would say. But then I suspect they wouldn't want me to talk to you."

"I think we'd feel more comfortable if you were cuffed," she said. "Precautions, you know."

Caleb laughed. "I certainly want you to be comfortable." He held his hands in front of him.

"Behind your back," Brownley said. "Turn around." Caleb gave Brownley a cold, thin smile and acquiesced. Brownley cuffed him and resumed his position.

"Feel safer now?" Caleb asked him. Brownley holstered his weapon, but kept his hand on the grip.

Kes stepped back to clear a path. "Down the hall. I'll tell you when to make a left." She noted Caleb's head turn slightly to take in each room he passed.

"Stop," Kes said. "Through that door."

He stepped into the interview room.

"Take a seat in the back corner."

Kes could feel his patience and control as he sat. He made her wait.

She set her phone between them and pushed record. Brownley, with his hand on his weapon, stayed at the door.

"Feel free to take a break, you must be tired. It's late. Must be past your bedtime," Caleb said to him.

Kes pulled his attention to her. "I was talking to your brother earlier."

"Were you?" Caleb's eyes sharpened. He smiled, a false smile. He seemed disappointed in her.

"I told him you were coming in to see me."

"And what did he say?" It felt like he was testing her.

"Nothing," she said. "He's never said anything."

He leaned back. "I like how we begin with small talk, Kes. Like friends." He pondered her as though trying to decide if she was worth his time. "People think my brother's either stupid or deaf, because he doesn't talk. They think he's mute, but he talks all the time if you listen."

Kes remained quiet. He wanted her to listen.

"Did you know he's an amazing tracker? He knows every-thing about the woods. Animals aren't afraid of him. They come right up. Birds, foxes, coyotes, wolves, bears and deer, of course. He's always been like that. He's never needed words." His eyes narrowed. "He's managed just fine, even after they cut out his tongue." He watched and waited for her to catch up. "He was eleven. You didn't know that did you, Kes? He's good at keeping it to himself."

Nothing in his body language shifted. His voice was flat, emotionless. Kes tried not to blink, but she did. "How did he learn to read the woods?"

"Ask me what you really want to know," Caleb parried.

"How did you survive after the fire at the school?"

"We ran, wandered around in circles for a few of days. We didn't know shit then. Stumbled upon a rabbit in a snare. Ate it right there. The blood was warm. Best thing we had ever tasted. We followed the traplines after that, acquired a taste for raw meat. We didn't want to make a fire and attract attention. We were so bit up by mosquitoes and horseflies we hardly recog-nized each other. One day, we were sleeping under an old pine.

There were impressions where other animals had lain before us. We woke to the sound of a rifle cocking."

"Barkley Smith," she said.

"Bark." He smiled, and the smile was true. "He took us in. Wanted nothing from us. Taught us how to survive. He was hard, but fair. He showed us how to lay lines, trap, hunt, and skin our catch. He taught us to think like animals. No guilt, no remorse—just action. I think that time with Bark might have been what happy feels like."

"Why didn't you stay?"

His eyes went cold again. "We wanted to get away from this place. You can understand that. When we were old enough and knew enough, we took what we had and headed north. Good money up north. Set ourselves up as guides for rich Americans. Let them kill old and diseased animals to make them feel like big men."

"Why come back?"

"Bark gave us a home, gave us the land. We thought maybe the ghosts would be gone, but they were still walking around town. It was time something was done about it, don't you think?"

"What did you think would happen afterwards? That you and your brother would just slip away and disappear in the woods?"

"Why not? We had before." He glanced up to the surveillance camera. "But my brother always had a softness to him. He wanted to mark the occasions, so the boys under the apple tree would know." He looked back to her. "They're not the only boys in that ground, Kes. My brother put up the crosses. That's all he did."

She didn't take his bait. She kept the focus on the present. Five brutalized corpses. "It's hard to imagine one man was able to restrain, move, and stage all those bodies and be in multiple places at the same time."

"And yet, all you have is me," he said. "And you only have me because I'm telling you."

He leaned forward. "Mason's innocent. He was their victim. He was beautiful back then, that's what they said. *Beautiful.* Do you know what they did to beautiful boys? He'd come back bleeding."

"And you?" she asked.

"I wasn't beautiful." He straightened. "They knew they couldn't break me. They tried, but I didn't give a fuck. I wasn't fun to play with."

She held the child's lie that had allowed him to survive what had made him into this man. His eyes hardened. He looked to Brownley again. "Did you get all that?"

Caleb turned back to Kes. "Are you tired, Kes? I'm tired." He sighed. "It's over now and I'm tired." His pupils were pin-point sharp. "I can see you haven't been sleeping well either, Kes. And those bruises and cuts. It's been a hard go for you. I see the pain in your eyes. The kind of pain you sometimes need to numb."

She held his stare. *Look*, she thought. *Look as deep as you want. Find all my secrets, because I don't give a fuck either.*

He smiled and shut his eyes. "Can I see my brother now? He's been caged long enough. Wild animals are driven mad in cages." When he opened his eyes, she saw only weariness and sorrow. The sorrow of a small boy.

"It's over, Kes."

XLI.

KES AND BROWNLEY ESCORTED CALEB TO THE HOLDING CELLS. THEY maintained a six-foot distance behind him, Brownley never letting down his guard.

"Stop," Kes said as they approached. On seeing his brother, Mason rose and stepped towards the bars. He was smiling and his eyes were watering.

"Hi, brother," Caleb said.

Mason made a guttural sound and Kes could see the stump of his tongue.

"Face the wall," she said. "I'm removing your belt."

Caleb, his cheek pressed to the wall, kept his eyes locked on his brother.

"Me and you always, right?"

Mason moaned something unintelligible.

"I promised."

Caleb bowed his head to the bars, as though relieved.

Kes reached around his torso and unclasped the buckle, tugged the belt loose, and tossed it behind Brownley. She looked to his workboots. They didn't have laces.

"I came prepared." Caleb said.

"Step to the back of the cell," Kes ordered Mason, who looked to his brother.

"It's okay," Caleb said, and Mason stepped back.

"If either moves, shoot Mason," she said to Brownley. "Turn around."

She had to look up to Caleb. If she'd seen him in the street, she might have thought he was a nice-looking man and admired his calm, confident presence. But his eyes were deadened. They reminded her of the eyes of a captive wolf she had seen in a zoo with her father. The broken creature had distressed her so much that she had burst into tears.

"What are you looking for, Detective?" Caleb asked.

She held his eyes, searching for what remained of a human being. This man who had systematically hunted and tortured his prey.

"You won't find it," he said.

She opened Cell Door 2.

"I'd rather be with my brother," he said.

"It doesn't work that way."

He smiled, as though it were a game, and stepped into the cell. She locked it behind him.

"Keys," she said to Brownley, who tossed them to her. "Back to the door," she directed Caleb.

He locked eyes with Mason. "It's going to be okay," he said.

She reached between the bars, removed the cuffs, and stepped back.

"Are we done?' he said.

"Yes."

Caleb and Mason stepped towards each other and met at the middle. They pressed their foreheads to the bars, and their fingers locked around cold steel. She couldn't hear what Caleb was murmuring, but his brother was nodding and responding with unintelligible sounds. He was crying.

She turned to Brownley, who looked as rumpled as his suit. This case had aged him. "Let the captain know."

Brownley stepped away.

When Kes first saw the holding cells at her father's pre-cinct as a righteous teenager, she'd accused him of cruelty. She thought he'd tell her that the guilty deserved to be punished. Instead, he had quietly said, *When you put a man in a cage, he'll act like a man in a cage.*

She watched the brothers embrace and could feel only their love. She didn't let herself imagine what would happen once they were separated. They didn't have the evidence to hold Mason. He would be released. But to what? What would his world be without his brother?

She had seen enough. She headed down the hall and as soon as she was out of sight, she pressed against the wall to suppress the surge of emotions—her fear, her pain, her revulsion, the terrible things she had seen—trying to claw their way out of her heart. She breathed in and out. She had got them. She had done her job. She felt no relief.

She stepped into the observation room and checked the camera. The brothers were still at the bars but had stepped apart. Only their hands clasped steel and flesh. Caleb was talking and laughing, like he was telling a story. Then the men's demeanour changed, became sombre and sad. Mason bowed his head to the bars and Caleb's fingers reached through to touch his cheek. Mason tilted his head, exposing his neck.

In that moment, Kes saw all the pieces fitting together. Caleb entering the station pulling open the door with his left hand. The knots at the crime scenes tied by a right-handed man. Spence patting him down. Caleb's arms held high above his head. A taller man than Spence. Spence starting the search just below his wrists. Brownley cuffing him. His right hand closing into a fist, slightly bent as the cuffs locked. The tilt of his hands to cup his wrists as she uncuffed him.

She ran from the room shouting for Brownley and fumbling for the cell keys. She rounded the corner to see the syringe slip from inside Caleb's right sleeve.

"Stop!" she yelled as he pressed his forehead to Mason's, his thumb on the plunger. She thought she heard someone say *I love you*. But the words were thick and tongueless. Brownley was shouting, "Step away!" The lock clicked and she swung open the door.

Caleb looked back at her, his eyes gleaming not with grief, but with an animal's instinctive certainty of a kill. He pressed down on the syringe.

A shot boomed, shattering her ears. The brothers gripped each other tight. Both momentarily suspended. The syringe empty. Caleb clutched Mason's shirt as his brother's body relaxed, guiding him gently to the floor. His eyes already empty of life. Caleb's knees crumpled. Blood trickled from his mouth and stained his side. A hunter's kill, straight through the heart. His hands dropped and he tipped forward, his still body kneeling before his brother.

Kes's ears were ringing. Far off, she could hear someone shouting.

There was the smell of smoke in the air. Someone was running forward—Spence? Brownley's weapon was pointed to the floor. He was saying something over and over. Puck, in civilian clothes, was charging down the hall. There was blood spilling around her feet.

All she could think about was the deer leaping and how beautiful it was just before it hit the tripwire.

EPILOGUE

THE BOW OF THE OLD LOBSTER BOAT LIFTED AND FELL WITH THE SWELLS. The wind was cool, the chill of spring mingling with the fog, but it felt cleansing on Kes's face. The ocean was a grey-green and spindrifts spilled from the crests. The boat passed the last headland and she could see only open sea ahead. It was exhilarating to feel so small in its expanse.

She looked back to the bridge and Captain Phil nodded to her, then fixed his gaze on the horizon. She was grateful he hadn't asked any questions when she arrived at the wharf. Simply told her to untie the lines and come aboard.

Kes closed her eyes and breathed in salt. She hadn't had a pill in two days. Or a drink. She had filed her reports and was facing an internal review when she got back to the city. It could be the only mark on her career. She had asked herself a hundred times if she had known what would happen. She still couldn't answer.

She had sat with her team. Helped them take down the board and pack up the evidence boxes. It had been quiet, each of them wrestling, in their own way, with what had transpired. Spence had offered to resign, feeling responsible for missing the syringe in the pat down, but Puck had refused his request.

Brownley had put in for a leave of absence. He and Susan were taking a vacation. It would be their first. Susan was wearing an engagement ring, and Chester was to be best man. Brownley had been cleared of the shooting. It was deemed an appropriate use of force. He was ordered to see a trauma psychologist, which he didn't feel he needed, but he'd left work twenty minutes early the day of his first appointment to make sure he wouldn't be late. Afterwards he said it wasn't so bad, and requested Wednesday mornings off for the next month to keep seeing the "talk doc."

Harrison, she was certain, would receive a Detective Constable offer soon. She and Puck had given strong recommendations on his behalf. His son was coming home for the summer. When he told Kes this, he was smiling, and she could see the young man he had once been, when he laughed more and anything was possible.

I'm the only one, she thought, *who doesn't know what's next.*

She breathed in and smelled brine. She could taste salt on her lips. Feel the thrum of the engine vibrating in her chest. Underneath the sound of the boat was a faint, high-pitched ringing in her left ear. Tinnitus from the gunshot. The doc said it might dissipate, and it had certainly lessened, but there was the possibility of hearing loss. Time would always tell.

Like this case. An investigation into the school had been opened; the local reporter was writing an exposé for a national paper. The guilty would be named. Kes hoped other survivors would step forward. That maybe there could still be justice. If not justice, then at least their stories finally told and heard. *There can be power in speaking your truth, maybe even healing.* She needed to believe that. Perhaps that was the best justice could be. Time would tell.

She tried to find her balance as the boat gently rolled and dipped, but had to keep adjusting her footing as she stepped out of rhythm. Her team had been kind to her. When she was ready to leave, all three had lined up and shook her hand. They handed her a small box containing half a dozen of Susan's fresh muffins, a deer carving that Chester had made, and a ballcap—Harrison's idea—with *Crusher* embroidered on the peak.

She felt like she had failed. They assured her she had not. Even Puck had offered her absolution and written the review board, defending and extolling her invaluable service, her exceptional conduct solving multiple cases and unearthing major crimes reaching back decades. On his way out the door, finally heading to his beloved golf course, he'd said, "Hope we don't see you around here again, Kes. But if anything comes up, I'll be asking for you."

She didn't know what her father would have said. She replayed the last words he had spoken, when his body was hollowed with disease and his voice a mere husk.

Stay the course.

Kes let herself be rocked, gave herself over to the sway of the boat and water, and stopped fighting the roll until she could no longer feel the movement beneath her. Until she and water and boat moved as one.

Stay the course. She felt her own skin rejuvenating, shedding the coarse hardness of something wild and amoral. She sloughed it from her, felt the fibres tearing away, leaving barbs in her heart. She knew she couldn't separate herself from it. Not completely. Remnants would remain stitched in hidden places.

The engine slowed and then shut down altogether. She stood in a silence that reached far beyond her. The boat continued to lift and fall like a heartbeat.

She opened her eyes and filled herself with light and sea and sky. Everything else was left behind. The wind teared her eyes, but that wasn't true. The boat was still and there wasn't any wind.

Her phone chirped and she answered, "Hi, baby...Mommy has missed you so much..."

In that moment, Kes felt only what she could describe as happy. Soon, she would be back.

ACKNOWLEDGEMENTS

THIS WRITER HAS JUST WRITTEN THE FINAL WORD, END, WHICH could not have been reached without the encouragement and assistance of the following people:

Editor Whitney Moran, who kept her aim at improving the story and supporting Kes at all costs. Terrilee Bulger, Kate Watson, Olivia Ingraham, and all the fine folk at Nimbus & Vagrant Press who made Kes a reality.

Quinn. Ebullient, astute, and supportive.

Early readers Natalie, Jo, Lana, Dan, Ellen, and Noah, who generously gave their time, knowledge, and shared their impressions. Your enthusiasm continued to fuel the process.

Patrick Moran, who helped set Kes straight on certain issues of protocol.

And finally, to Annie. Who reminded the writer of how important it is to take a walk every day...and to whom this book is dedicated.

Thank you all.